CAROLYN SUMM

CHILD OF SECRETS FROM AFAR

Who is after their adopted daughter?

This is a work of fiction. Similarities to real people, places, or events are entirely coincidental.

CHILD OF SECRETS FROM AFAR

First edition. February 14, 2024.

ISBN: 979-8224608546

Written by Carolyn Summer Quinn.

Child of Secrets From Afar

By Carolyn Summer Quinn

Books By Award-Winning Author Carolyn Summer Quinn

———◦———

Cozy Mysteries:
Child of Secrets From Afar
The Hollywood Backlash Moon
A Charm Without a Chain
Vanished on the Vaudeville Circuit
Backstabbed on Broadway
Cloudy with a Chance of Answers
The Final Comeuppance

———◦———

Nonfiction Biography of the Theatrical Legend
Who Inspired the Musical GYPSY:
Mama Rose's Turn: The True Story of America's
Most Notorious Stage Mother

———◦———

Middle Grade Children's Books:
Now and Forevermore Arabella
Keep Your Songs in Your Heart:
A Story of Friendship and Hope During World War II

<u>Dedication:</u>

My uproarious dad Frank Quinn's little brother Joseph (1932-2023) was, by all accounts, a funny kid when they were growing up, along with their equally hilarious little brother Jimmy, in the predominantly Irish "Keighryhead" neighborhood of Elizabeth, NJ. It's no wonder these three kids had such a great sense of humor. Their mother, my Grandma Claire, was born hilarious and stayed that way. My father used to tell me all kinds of stories about the goofy stunts he, Joe and Jimmy used to get into, especially about the funny faces they'd make in church. Dad later taught those to me.

When Uncle Joe grew up, my dad chose him to be my godfather. Uncle Joe was already a lawyer when I arrived on the scene, then became a judge, then topped that by getting appointed to be a member of the Colorado State Supreme Court. After that I always called him "Justice Joe" whenever I saw him at family events. Ultimately, he rose even further in his career. The fun-loving little boy from Elizabeth retired as none other than Joseph R. Quinn, Chief Justice of the Colorado State Supreme Court.

To me, Justice Joe was always a whole lot more than just his wonderful collection of titles. He was also a good husband to my Aunt Olga, the father of five, and one of the most decent people I've ever been lucky enough to have known. It was phenomenal to have him as my godfather.

So Justice Joe, this one's for *you!*

Courage is fire, and bullying is smoke.
—Benjamin Disraeli

———◉———

Opportunity makes a thief.
—Francis Bacon

———◉———

There was never a good war, or a bad peace.
—Benjamin Franklin

Chapter One

<u>Unaccounted For</u>
April 5, 1975

The day when everything started going awry was supposed to be one of the best days of our lives.

But it didn't work out that way.

My husband Jonathan and I had applied a year earlier to adopt a little girl called Binh from Vietnam. She was seven years old and had been living in an orphanage for most of her life. There had been one delay with this adoption after another. But all of a sudden she was due to arrive on the first Operation Babylift flight from Saigon to California that would be arriving later that day. Finally, after waiting so long, the child was going to be on American soil and it would be happening within hours.

Or so we thought.

My husband and I, along with our daughter Holly, age nine, were hoping to arrange for airline tickets later that morning so we could fly to San Francisco to pick her up. The plan was to stay there for a few days, see the sights, and then fly home to Indiana.

It was either that, or we would have to wait until Binh was escorted to the Midwest on a flight to Chicago, which meant waiting a few more days, or even a week, to get her. We could easily drive there to meet her.

However, I didn't like that idea so much. None of us did. It would be so much nicer for the little orphan girl if we could get to California as soon as possible. Seven years was long enough for that child to wait in an orphanage for a family. She shouldn't have to arrive in California, find there was no one there to meet her, and have to wait even longer to find out she had a family at last.

It had been hard for all of us to get to sleep the night before. We already felt as though it had taken forever for Binh to join our family. Her new room was ready, painted pink and white, with frilly curtains on the windows that overlooked our apple tree in the backyard, and a collection of new dolls and stuffed animals on her bed, just waiting for her to love them.

There had been all sorts of delays with this adoption, our first. Our daughter Holly was our own child. Jonathan and I had tried for years to give her a sibling but without success. We hadn't known it would take so long, but several people who were more in the know about Vietnam than we were had told us the bureaucrats there tended to play by their own rules and did things on their own sweet time. Jonathan had seen a little of that when he had been in Vietnam with the Air Force eleven years earlier, in 1964, which was when he'd first became aware of the situation with the orphans over there in the first place, but even he was astounded at how much red tape was involved with this adoption.

There had been war and conflicts in Vietnam for decades, most recently, and infamously, with communists from the North of the country fighting the capitalists from the South. American troops had been sent there in the 1960s to try and stop the communists. The United States of America had been at a fever pitch against communism ever since a married couple, who were spies, had stolen the secrets to make our atomic bombs back in the 1950s and handed the plans to the Soviet Union. My country was convinced that the "commies" were out for world domination and that stopping them any way we could was a top American priority.

The Vietnam War turned out to be a fight we weren't able to help the South Vietnamese win. The American forces had finally given up the fight and pulled out of there in January of 1973.

The North Vietnamese commies waited.

And waited. They bided their time.

And in March of 1975, they invaded, and began their takeover, of South Vietnam.

It may sound unpatriotic of us, since America had gotten so involved in Vietnam's war, but my husband and I couldn't have cared less about the North or the South or the commies or the capitalists. We weren't at all concerned with stolen atomic bomb plans or world domination plots. We just wanted to get that little orphan girl, Binh, out of there, away from the war zone, have her home with us, and legally adopt her. She'd be our daughter, Holly's little sister. It was all going to turn out like a Norman Rockwell painting, I thought. Two little girls hunting together for Easter eggs, going trick-or-treating in their Halloween costumes, eating turkey at the Thanksgiving Day table, and opening presents on Christmas morning.

Silly me.

Always the optimist.

Yet it was a worthy dream if ever there was one.

Meanwhile, the more advances that the North Vietnamese troops made in the way of taking over the South, town by town, city by city, the more concerned the United States government became over the thousands of Vietnamese orphans. Quite a lot of them were half-American orphans, the children of American soldiers and Vietnamese girls. That made them "our" kids, or at least, halfway our kids, so to speak, so President Gerald Ford arranged for planes to bring them to our shores.

On the morning of April 5, a phone call woke us up.

Binh had been on the very first Operation Babylift flight out of the country.

It had crashed in a rice paddy.

There were a lot of miraculous survivors. That was the good news.

But there had been a lot of deaths as well.

And Binh?

She was currently "unaccounted for."

That's what Marianne Bigsby, our contact in Chicago from our international adoption agency, was telling me on the phone at six-fifteen in the morning. Binh wasn't among the dead, but she wasn't one of the survivors, either.

I had a hard time with that one. She wasn't dead in the crash but she also wasn't on the plane?

Or was she?

The whole thing didn't make one ounce of sense to me. "Either she was traveling on that plane," I insisted to Marianne, "or she wasn't. What was it?"

"There's so much confusion over there in Vietnam at the moment," Marianne told me in a tone clearly meant to try and appease my worries, but it only came out sounding frazzled. The poor woman. We probably weren't the only phone call she had to make. "We're simply not sure, Belinda. Binh was supposed to be on the plane, but who knows?"

"Who knows?" I repeated indignantly, my heart breaking for the child who was meant to be my daughter. "How can it be that nobody knows what happened with regards to a little seven-year-old girl?"

"I assure you, we've got people on the ground in Nam and they're trying to find out for you, for us. Anything could have happened. Maybe Binh had a fever or something and the orphanage people decided to hold her back from this particular flight and put her on a later one."

"Or maybe," I all but wailed, "she's already lying dead from the crash in the rice paddy!"

"Pray," Marianne told me. "Just pray, Belinda. That's about all anyone can do right now. And if Binh didn't make it, there's no need to worry. You're already approved for an adoption. We can match you with another little girl to take Binh's place, if it comes to that. There are at least a thousand kids coming here from over there who are going to need a good home. I'll call you again later."

I hung up the phone in total disbelief. No need to worry? Match us with another little girl to take Binh's place? What did Marianne Bigsby think these children were, anyway, interchangeable? This one's dead so we'll send you some other one? I was so mad my hands were shaking.

Not that I wouldn't take another little girl if the worst had happened to Binh. I would, and in a heartbeat. Another girl would still be a child in need of a home, a family and love.

It was just the idea of Binh being replaceable that was driving me nuts. No child is.

We were planning on calling Binh by a more Americanized name, "Bonnie." It would, we hoped, make for a smoother transition to America for her if she had a more American name. Her full name was going to be Bonnie Binh O'Malley. I loved the sound of it. Binh meant "peaceful" and Bonnie meant "pretty." We were even planning on nicknaming her "Pretty Peaceful O'Malley."

We had put so much love and joy in planning for her arrival...and now this.

Jonathan got up and I relayed the whole horrific story to him. He held my trembling hands in his until the shaking stopped. "Don't blame Marianne," he said, looking at me with worried green eyes. "She's obviously got her hands full this morning with having to call people up and tell them about this plane crash. I wouldn't want her to have job today and neither would you."

"Even so," I sighed. "Poor Binh."

"Hopefully she's just coming in on a later flight. Meanwhile, I wonder what we should do," he added. "Try to go on to San Francisco like we planned? Or stay here and wait for news?"

"We were going to go as a family, all three of us," I said, thinking out loud as I spoke, "but if we don't know when Binh or another child for us might be landing in Frisco, we should probably just wait. What if Binh shows up but it takes a week? Or longer? We don't want to be staying out there, waiting indefinitely. Holly would have to miss too much school."

Jonathan sighed. "You're right. Let's just wait this out and see what happens."

Going to California would have beaten the heck out of sitting around at home and waiting for the phone to ring, I thought. I'd been so looking forward to meeting Bonnie and also getting a few days to see the sights of San Francisco. Yet what choice did we really have?

Chapter Two

Lotus Flower

The situation in San Francisco could not have been crazier, according to Marianne's regular telephone updates. She was there, along with the workers from several other adoption agencies as well as kindhearted local volunteers, welcoming the children as they arrived.

Some of the babies and children showed up with medical conditions and were taken straight to area hospitals. The rest were brought to The Presidio, an old army base that was being used as a temporary weigh station while they either waited for their adoptive parents to show up or were escorted onto additional flights to be brought to their new homes.

There was a lot to arrange for the children's welcome. Most of the kids arrived with nothing but the clothes on their backs, whatever they had been wearing when they left their orphanages, since quite a lot of the departures from those places were made in haste. After all, Saigon was still falling to the communists all around them as the children and their caregivers made their way to Tan Son Nhat Airport.

I could only imagine the chaos, not to mention the terror, of those little ones as they left their conquered country.

Marianne Bigsby and the others at the Presidio arranged to give the new arrivals some new clothes, to feed them well, and even ensured each child received a toy. They also set up a makeshift English class for the ones who didn't leave to go to their new homes immediately.

She hoped to see Binh every time a new group of children arrived, but time and again, the little girl simply failed to show up. Had she never gotten on the plane that crashed? Had she been on it and died?

Or was there another possibility? Might the child have been onboard, survived the crash, and maybe either managed to miraculously walk away or been found by someone who simply took her home with them?

The third possibility wasn't as unlikely as it might have seemed on the surface. We heard that debris from that plane was spread out for a mile. That was all over the news. Survivors might have been anywhere along that mile.

It could happen. But had it happened to Binh?

Two full weeks after the day when we had meant to fly to San Francisco to get our daughter, Marianne Bigsby called me again. "There's still no sign of her," she said miserably. "But there is another little girl, a beautiful child, who has yet to be assigned to a family. Her name is Lien and she's eight years old. That's L-I-E-N, pronounced like *lee-en*. Not like a lien on a house. It means 'lotus flower.' We think she's fully Vietnamese, same as Binh was, or is. She doesn't appear to be one of those children with an American soldier as a father. And, oh, Belinda, she's quite despondent, this child is. Very sad at being brought here, though we can't figure out why. She won't answer our questions and tell us, not even through the translators. And while she doesn't say it, and tries not to show it, we think the more she sees other kids leaving with their new parents, the worse she feels. I think she'd be perfect for you and Jonathan, and with your upbeat personalities, you'd both be perfect for her. What do you say?"

"Do you think there's no hope at all for us ever finding Binh?" I had to ask before answering.

"At this point? I'm so sorry, but yes. I think it's time to admit defeat."

That was the last thing I wanted to do, although it seemed as if there wasn't really much of a choice. If the child was gone, one way or the other, she was gone.

"Let me talk it over with Jonathan," I said with a heavy heart, "and I'll call you back."

"No, let me give you an hour and I can call you when I get back to my hotel. It's a madhouse here, we've got another planeload coming in any minute, and I'm not by a phone."

"I can just imagine."

"No, actually," Marianne said with an ironic smile in her voice, "you probably can't."

Binh, Binh, I thought desperately. My little Binh. How can we possibly just give up on you? Are you really and truly gone?

But then, if she was, there was this other child, this sad little Lien. This eight-year-old who was currently feeling so miserable in the Presidio.

In the end Jonathan and I didn't hesitate for a minute. We decided we'd adopt Lien, and finally made our plans to fly, along with Holly, to San Francisco to get her.

———— ◉ ————

Jonathan and I had been honest, right from the start, with Holly about the fact that Binh was missing.

For one thing the plane crash was all over the television news and the newspapers, too. There was no way to keep our nine-year-old from hearing about it. She told us it was even discussed in school, in her fourth grade classroom. It made our Holly unnaturally subdued because she was an exuberant little girl.

Every night we had prayed for Binh. On Sunday at Mass we each lit a candle for her, hoping God in his heaven would hear our prayers and bring her safely to this country.

Now we had to tell her that Binh wasn't coming after all.

Lien was.

Holly was full of questions as my brother, her Uncle Alan, who was a police detective, drove us to the airport.

"What does she look like? Why haven't we seen a picture of her? And what are we going to do about her name?" She asked, all in a rush, while bouncing on the back seat next to me. Jonathan rode with Alan in the front.

"That's a good question about her name," Alan commented. "You said on the phone last night that it's pronounced like *lee-en*, Sis?"

"Yes," I said. "It means lotus."

"Should we call her Lotus, then?" Holly asked.

I tried out the sound of it. "Lotus O'Malley? I don't think that works all that well."

"It sounds," Alan laughed, "like a gal who should be arrested for solicitation."

"What's that?" Holly wanted to know.

"Never mind," Jonathan told her.

Meanwhile, I was thinking about our new daughter's name all the way to the airport. Finally, when we got there, I said, "I've got it. We can call Lien 'Liana.' Liana O'Malley. It's pretty, it flows well, and it's close enough to her real name that she should be comfortable with it."

With that, I figured, we were ready for Lien-Liana, the little girl originally named after a lotus blossom, to join our family.

Or were we?

Chapter Three

<u>Guess What?</u>

I had just enough time before we left for San Francisco to look up the significance of lotus flowers in a guidebook on Vietnam that I had bought weeks earlier.

We weren't, of course, going to Vietnam, not at this point. Maybe someday. Not now while the war was still raging. But the book, at least, gave me some information I'd never had before about the country.

The lotus blossom was their national flower. I had never known it before, not being a botanist, but lotuses rose from the mud every day at dawn. They were considered a symbol of purity, as a result. They were also a symbol of transcendence, of man's ability to rise above situations.

I was thinking of this as our plane took off and we started on our journey to pick up our little lotus, Liana.

Our hotel in San Francisco was a large and luxurious one, complete with a gift shop. We hadn't yet checked into our room when Holly ran across the lobby to the shop, saw there were teddy bears in the window, and begged me to buy one for Liana.

"That's a great idea," I said. We went inside while Jonathan dealt with the front desk and check-in. We came back out again with a blue and white bear with a cute grin on his stuffed little face.

"She's going to love this," my daughter predicted.

We were tired, and already on the way to becoming a bit jet-lagged, but still eager to get a move on. We wanted to go straight to the Presidio to get our new daughter and bring her back to the hotel with us.

It was a short cab ride away. The Presidio was a former military base with sparkling white buildings that had red tile roofs. It was located right near the Golden Gate Bridge, which turned out to be not golden, exactly, but more like a rusty orange. This was, I said, a great first place to bring these children. So pretty.

Once we got inside of the building where the children were being temporarily housed, I could tell at once that Marianne's descriptions of the chaos had been spot on. Another flight of orphans had just arrived, most looking rather lost and bedraggled, some crying, some playful and curious, a few already running around.

I had met Marianne Bigsby before and knew she was a dark-haired middle-aged lady and had warm brown eyes, but there was no sign of her in the building. Instead another representative from the same adoption agency, a very tall, big-boned woman, blonde and blue, who reminded me of illustrations I'd once seen somewhere of Vikings, brought us into a small room and said to wait there and she'd be right back with Lien.

Holly was practically jumping for joy. Jonathan and I sat next to one another, holding hands.

The Viking came back, leading a small girl, one who looked more like six years old than eight, by the hand. Lien was, just as Marianne had said, a beautiful child. She had shoulder-length straight dark hair and large brown eyes over a cupid's bow mouth. What a little sweetie. That was my first thought.

Though I noticed her cheeks were stained with tears.

"Liana!" Jonathan and I said in unison.

The little girl looked around, probably wondering, "Liana, who's that?" She didn't know what we had renamed her yet.

"You're my sister," Holly told the confused child. She ran over to her with the stuffed bear, handed it to her, and hugged her.

Lien stood there woodenly, as if she didn't know what to do with this kid, this stranger. Surely she also didn't have any idea what the English word "sister" meant.

"We're your new parents," I tried to tell Lien. I pointed to myself. "Mommy." I gestured, in turn, to Jonathan. "Daddy." And finally to Holly. "Big sister."

The child responded with a blank look, though her eyes had brightened just the tiniest bit. I could tell she was curious about us. Maybe she was even glad we were there, that a family had come, at last, for her. She just wasn't going to reveal it yet.

"Can you get a translator for us?" Jonathan asked the agency woman. "This poor child can't understand a thing we're trying to say to her."

"Of course," the lady said, "one moment and I'll be right back with one."

Lien looked upset when the woman left the room, as though she didn't want to be left alone with us. We were still strangers to her, after all. She'd probably had enough of dealing with people she'd never seen before during these last few confusing days.

"It's okay, little one," I told her gently, hoping that I could calm this kid with my tone of voice, even if the meaning of my words escaped her.

"She's so small," Holly commented. "She doesn't look old enough to be eight."

"They're smaller people, the Vietnamese," said Jonathan. "Generally, they are, anyway. Not as big as Americans." He knew a lot about them from having been over there when he was with the Air Force back.

Lien was looking at the bear, which Holly held out to her. "It's for you, Liana."

Liana took the blue bear in her arms, touched the big red bow around its neck, and even gave the tiniest hint of a smile. She also said something to us, but of course only Jonathan understood what it was.

"She just said thank you," he reported. "But that's about the extent of what I remember how to say in her language, yes, no, hello, and thank you."

I wanted to scoop this lovely child up, hold her nice and tight on my lap, and tell her I already loved her, but that would have been too much too soon. I didn't want to frighten my brand new daughter.

The tall blonde gal came back, along with the translator, an elderly Vietnamese lady with graying hair. The Swedish-looking woman finally introduced herself as Solveig and the translator as Huong.

"Please tell this wonderful girl that we're her new family," I all but begged Huong.

She said as much, or at least I assume she did, to Lien.

Lien looked startled. She said something back, *"Khong,"* followed by a long string of words, and it was obvious that she was speaking in protest.

"Khong," Jonathan said to me in an undertone. "I remember that one from when I was in the service over there. That means 'no.'"

My heart sank. Didn't this orphan want us for her family? We certainly wanted her.

On the other hand, again, we were total strangers, and Americans to boot. Almost all of the Americans in Vietnam had been soldiers, military. Maybe she feared us, as a result. Maybe she had seen our people fighting with hers in battle, even. In that case, of course she'd be hesitant to go home with us. I mean, who could tell what her past experiences had been?

The child continued talking with Huong. It looked like she was desperately trying to explain something. My heart went out to her without even knowing the details. What had her so worked up? The two of them continued talking back and forth for five agonizingly long minutes.

Huong finally turned to us. "I think this one's confused. She keeps saying she can't leave yet, that she needs to stay here so she can go home. It doesn't make any sense. She's from the Star of the Sea Orphanage, and I keep telling her it's been shut down, that all the orphans are here now, and all the children will be getting new families, but she doesn't seem to understand. She wants to talk with the orphanage director, Sister Elizabeth, but she isn't here." Huong shrugged helplessly. "I'm trying my best to explain everything to her but it isn't working."

"Oh, Sister Elizabeth isn't here. She arrived with a medical problem and had to go to the hospital the other day, not long after the plane she and Lien were on landed. And quite a lot of these children here are confused," Solveig explained. "It's been far too abrupt for them, this whole Operation Babylift situation. One minute they're secure in their orphan's institutions, even though that isn't ideal. They're used to it there, you see. The next thing they know, they're out of there, put on a plane, stop off in the Philippines, and finally they're here. Most of them don't seem to understand any of it."

Then you, or someone in charge here, should take the time to explain it to them, I thought to myself but didn't say out loud. You have translators. These children, like Lien, aren't so young that they couldn't understand all this if only they were told the details.

"Please tell her," Jonathan said to Huong, "that she's going to be adopted by us. That I'm her dad, Belinda here is her mom, and Holly will be her big sister. That from now on, we're her family. That we live in Emerson, Indiana, and can't wait to take her home with us."

Huong went into his explanation with the little girl. She still seemed to be unhappy with the idea, stubbornly shaking her head.

"Tell her it's already been decided," Solveig finally instructed Huong forcefully. "Tell her this is her family and she ought to be a little bit nicer to them since they've come such a long way to get here and meet her. And remind her, besides, that first impressions are lasting, so she ought to try making a good one."

I didn't think that approach would be the best way for this discombobulated child to start off with us as her new family, by getting a command from the Viking lady. But after hearing it, Lien looked at us with curiosity.

I held out my arms to her, and amazingly, she came forward, a little hesitantly, into my hug. Jonathan hugged her next. Holly patted her on the back. I took Lien onto my lap after that, and for a long time. She put her head on my shoulder and seemed to relax. Maybe she was tired. She had had a lot of changes to deal with just in getting here.

There were lots of forms for us to sign, and then we were ready to take her back to the hotel with us.

Solveig left the room once the paperwork was done. I asked Huong to explain to Lien about the hotel, and that in two days we'd be flying on an airplane to go home to Indiana. After that she would be home with us.

Lien said something to Huong.

"Oh, she's got some things that she wants to get," Huong told us. "Probably the pajamas and change of clothes that we gave her when she arrived, and a doll or whatever toy she received."

We walked with Lien to the big dormitory room where she retrieved a plastic bag of stuff that was sitting tucked under the covers of the cot she had been occupying. The child was a bit more friendly with us and opened the bag to show Holly that she had a new blouse in there, a pair of green slacks, the pajamas Huong mentioned, and two toys, a Holly Hobby doll and another one from Vietnam. How she had managed to get the Vietnamese doll out, onto the Babylift plane, and across the ocean to California was a mystery, but she had done it. The doll was about sixteen inches long and had a porcelain face and a cloth body. The doll was wearing what Huong told us was a traditional Vietnamese dress, a red and white *ao dai*. It was like a long red dress with a high mandarin collar over loose white slacks, very sleek and feminine and pretty. It also wore a conical hat on its head.

"She's lovely," I told Lien. Since she didn't understand, I smiled and gave her a thumbs up. That made the kid grin. It was the first time we'd seen her dazzling smile.

"Okay then," Jonathan said with a smile to Lien, "let's saddle up!"

That was when Marianne Bigsby, with her dark hair styled in curls, found us.

She looked distressed.

"Jonathan, Belinda, I'm so glad I caught you before you left. We need to talk." She looked at my daughter and said to Holly, "Why don't you and Lien go into the playroom for a little while? You can both have a snack in there."

Marianne had a good command of Vietnamese, having gone over there plenty of times on adoption agency business, and repeated this to Lien in her own language. Lien led Holly to the playroom.

"You're not going to believe this," Marianne said when the girls were gone from the dormitory. "But guess what? Binh just arrived on the latest plane."

Chapter Four

<u>We'll Take Both</u>

"Binh!" I exclaimed with delight. "She's here? She made it out in one piece?"

"She sure did," Marianne said apologetically, "and I'm so sorry! So very sorry."

"Why?" I asked. "This is incredibly good news!"

"The best," Jonathan agreed with his most handsome grin.

"But I jumped the gun with this other kid for you, this Lien," Marianne replied, distraught. "I had her introduced to you and everything. I suppose now you won't want to take her after all. You'll want Binh, as originally planned."

Jonathan and I looked at one another. His green eyes met my blue ones. In that moment, it was as if I could read his mind, and he could read mine.

"Well, I always wanted a big family," he said slowly.

"And ever since I found out I couldn't have more children after we had Holly, I've wanted her to have siblings," I added with a smile. "That's *siblings*, Marianne. Plural."

"We'll take them both," Jonathan told Marianne.

She looked astonished, but pleased, too. "This is wonderful!" She exulted.

"Now let's meet our Binh," I urged. "We've waited so long for her!"

"The poor kid had been feverish," Marianne told us. "It's why she was put on a later plane. They didn't want her to infect the other children."

It was back to the little room where we had met Lien. This time, the child who was led in by Solveig wasn't shy or reticent or protesting about anything. Little Binh, an adorable child easily recognizable from the photos we'd been sent of her with her chin-length straight black hair and mischievous eyes, ran straight over to Jonathan and me with open arms. We'd sent her photos of us, too, so knew us right away. We three had a long group hug.

Someone had found Holly and Lien in the playroom and they came in to join us, with Holly over the moon when she saw Binh and recognized her from the photos of her that we'd been sent.

We asked Huong to tell the girls their new American names, Liana and Bonnie.

"I Bonnie," Binh smiled happily, pointing to herself. "I *Bonnie!*"

"Looks like this one will make a very easy adjustment," Solveig observed with a big toothy smile.

"She even speaks a little English already," Huong nodded.

Liana didn't seem half as enthusiastic. She just nodded, looking a bit resigned. She repeated, "Lee-ah-nah."

There were more forms to sign, receipts, I guess, for our taking possession of Bonnie. My relief at finding her here couldn't have been more enormous. The idea that this bubbly kid might have been killed in that horrific plane crash was more than I could handle. It would have haunted me my whole life, but now, I knew, it wouldn't. We were going to be bringing her home!

"Let me get Bonnie a change of clothes and a nightgown," Solveig said, "to take with you so that she has something for tonight and tomorrow. I'll be right back." She returned with the items in another plastic bag, and handed a Raggedy Ann doll to Bonnie, too.

"Here's you loot," she told the child.

"Loot loot," Bonnie repeated. Then she hugged me again, tightly, like she didn't ever want to let me go. This was a child who had waited a long time to be hugged.

"Did she bring anything with her like Liana did?" I couldn't help but ask. If she had, the last thing I wanted was for her to leave whatever she might have brought from her former life behind.

"No, nothing. Most of them came with nothing at all," said Solveig with a shrug.

"They won't," Jonathan declared, "have nothing for long." He carried both of the girls' bags and we were ready to go.

I noticed an odd Asian man as we left the Presidio just standing outside, leaning against a tree. He seemed to jump back and do a double-take when he saw us leaving the building, but that, I reasoned, had to be my imagination.

He was wearing aviator sunglasses and had a droopy mustache. There was also a scar on his left cheek, about an inch long, like the results of a slash. I wondered who he was. He looked Vietnamese, and if that was the case, they could have probably used his help inside, especially if he spoke English well enough to translate for the children.

Oh well. It really was none of my business.

I had two new daughters who were going to need a lot of love. I held both of their hands as we walked along.

"We'll go on a tour of San Francisco tomorrow," Jonathan was saying to Holly. "We'll see the sights, maybe ride a cable car, and go to Fisherman's Wharf. Would you like that?"

"You better believe it, I would," Holly answered with a grin.

We piled into a taxi to go back to the hotel, where we headed straight to the dining room for some dinner. Jonathan ordered hamburgers and French fries for all of us, followed by vanilla ice cream for dessert. All three kids devoured everything, Bonnie a bit more enthusiastically than Liana, with Holly demonstrating to the other two on how to make the best possible use of the ketchup.

I had to wonder what these two new children of mine were used to eating at home in Nam. I knew absolutely nothing about Vietnamese food. I was aware of only a tiny bit of information about their culture, and most of that I had gleaned from Jonathan's tales of his time over there in the service and that guidebook that mentioned the lotus blossoms. I was aware that the Vietnamese people were usually either Buddhists or Catholics and had no idea which religion the girls had been raised in, though Liana was from the Star of the Sea Orphanage and it had been run by nuns. Now that they were my kids I would need to find out more about their upbringing.

One step at a time, I told myself. My mind was going off in all directions, wondering what religion, if any, these girls had been raised in, or what their life had been like over there, and this was still our first dinner over here. It would have helped if someone like Huong had been along to translate tonight, but she wasn't.

Bonnie and Liana talked a lot to each other in Vietnamese, while Holly tried to teach them various words in English, spoon, fork, knife, table, cup. I hoped they picked up English pretty quickly. Communication was going to be something of a problem until they did. Yet I was sure that the love of their new family – us – would be able to help them conquer just about anything.

That was how naïve I was back then.

Naïve, yes, but very well-intentioned, just the same.

After dinner was over I realized that the few new clothing items Bonnie and Liana had been given at the Presidio were by no means all they would need at the moment. They had no underwear save for what they already wore, no jackets for the cool spring weather here or the even cooler temperatures they'd be facing once we got to Indiana, no change of socks, and nowhere near enough outfits in general. They didn't even have toothbrushes. I may have been near exhaustion by that point, with a touch of jet lag starting to sock in, yet asked Jonathan to watch the three girls in the hotel room while I went out to a nearby department store to get them some additional items.

It may have been a bit problematic for me to go out and shop at that point, when I just wanted to take a nice rest, but this was, I felt, a positive problem to have, this desire to outfit these kids who had practically nothing.

Especially compared to what the people of Saigon were going through at the moment, with the North Vietnamese military overrunning the city, my happy predicament was nothing. I was among the luckiest people on the planet in that particular point in time and I knew it. My husband was a prosperous businessman, the vice president of an Indianapolis advertising agency. I had once been a second grade teacher but now had the luxury of being a stay-at-home housewife. I'd also been fortunate enough to be in a position to take in two adorable orphans from Saigon.

I wasn't over there in Nam, cowering in fear of whatever might be about to happen next as the tanks rolled in.

The tanks. What on earth would it be like if I was a mother over there, with incoming tanks, soldiers and an invading army?

Well, I wasn't there, I was here, and I thanked God heartily for that. I was here, in California, safe in the land of the free and the home of the brave.

It was when I got to the department store, looked at the directory to find out where the children's clothes were, and saw the word BEDDING on the list that I remembered something else. We had Bonnie's room all set up for her, pink, white and perfect, but what about Liana? How would it look to her if when we went home, Bonnie had a beautiful bedroom waiting for her yet Liana didn't?

Alan, I thought, as I made my way to the children's clothing section. My brother Alan and his wife, Julie, could always be counted on in an emergency, and this counted as one, at least to me. They had keys to my house. They kept an eye on it whenever Jonathan, Holly and

I were away. I would call them once back at the hotel and ask them to please, please, *please*, get to a store, work a little magic, and transform the guest room into a little girl's bedroom for Liana as quickly as they possibly could. I would reimburse them for any cost they might lay out.

I got blouses for my new children, slacks, pajamas, socks, underwear, a pretty new dress for each, and cute little cardigan sweaters as well. I found myself adding Holly to the shopping list when I saw three powder blue winter jackets with white fake fur trim for sale that came in the right sizes for all three girls. They'd look like sisters in those for sure.

Well, maybe they wouldn't exactly look alike, with one blonde freckle-faced Irish-American child and two Vietnamese ones, but when people saw them coming down the street, one look and they'd know my girls were a unit. It might even ease their bonding.

Silly me.

I was so concerned, I realized much later, about all of the wrong things, like Americanizing the names, buying some identical clothing, and making the three kids into sisters. They were sisters by way of adoption, yes, but they were unrelated otherwise. Bonnie and Liana came with histories of their own. Would it have been better if I'd tried harder, right from the start, to learn all I could about where they came from, rather than trying to mold them right into American kids?

But what could I have done differently? It was this great humanitarian mission we adoptive parents felt like we had embarked upon, trying to give loving homes to these unfortunate homeless children, who had arrived from a violent war zone, yet. We could not easily communicate with them. That was the biggest hurdle we had to overcome in the beginning. Without a translator handy, it wasn't possible to easily discuss anything with these children, least of all their past histories. About all I knew was that both girls were considered to be one hundred percent Vietnamese and had not been fathered by

American GIs, but even that was a guess made by social workers at the adoption agency.

A quote I liked, one the late, great Martin Luther King had said, came to mind as I was waiting on the line to check out my purchases. "We may have all come on different ships but we're in the same boat now." That was the right idea. I was certain of it. We just had to proceed from there.

I wound up with four shopping bags of items to carry. It was lucky that I got a cab as easily as I did. Only when I was in it did I realize there was something else I had needed to get and failed to think of it in time. An extra suitcase was going to be needed to get all of these new outfits back to Indiana. I'd have to go back to the department store the next day.

Back in the hotel room, the three kids were sitting in front of the television set, watching *The Flintstones*. Jonathan had gotten sodas and popcorn for them, probably from room service, and they already struck me as a cohesive little group.

I wasn't prepared for the jubilation I was met with when the show ended and I revealed the new clothes to the children. All three of them were delighted, Holly with her new jacket and the other two with every purchase that I pulled out of the bags. I had to wonder what had gone on in the orphanages they came from. What had they normally been given to wear, rags, for God's sake? Other people's castoffs? In any event, I had a roomful of very happy kids that night.

I also managed to call my brother Alan before dropping off to sleep. His wife joined the call on the extension. "We're coming home with two girls, not one," I explained. "It's a long story. Bonnie Binh arrived just when we'd given up hope of her ever being located. We're also still taking the other child, Liana. She's very quiet but she's a lovely little girl. And we really need your help. Could you do what you can to make our sleek guest room over into a little girl's bedroom for Liana?"

Neither one hesitated. "Of course," Julie said.

"We're at your service, Sis," Alan assured me. "What do you want us to get?"

The guest room was painted a pale mint green. "Some toys and dolls, like the ones that are in Bonnie's room. A frilly bedspread and curtains for the windows. Maybe some pictures on the wall of children or carousels or something. Just make the room more kid friendly than it is at the moment." That guest room was done in an antique Art Deco style, which I loved, but it wouldn't be at all right for eight-year-old Liana.

"We're on it! We'll get everything tomorrow," Alan promised.

And that was that. I got my nightgown on, sat propped up on pillows on the bed, and fell asleep watching Jonathan and the kids laugh at another cartoon, thinking all was going to be right with my world.

I didn't think of that other quote. Or was it a cliché?

The one that said the best laid plans often go awry.

Chapter Five

<u>Weirder than Weird</u>

At two o'clock in the morning, Pacific Time, Liana cried out in her sleep.

Actually, to say she "cried out" wasn't exactly accurate. It was more like she let out a scream, poor kid.

What on earth was this?

The three kids were all asleep in the second queen-sized bed in our room, with Holly in the middle, out cold. Liana was on the side of her closest to the bed I shared with Jonathan. I sat on the edge of the bed and gently woke her up. She blinked and let out a long string of sentences in her own language that of course I could not understand.

Bonnie had been awakened by the disturbance as well, and so had Jonathan.

"What's wrong with her?" He asked. "She was screaming fit to rival a banshee."

"No idea," I said. "What is it, little one?" I asked the child.

No answer. She had no idea of what I'd just asked, but she reached for my hand and held on tight. Whatever is going on in that little head of hers, I thought, at least it seems as if she likes me.

I sat there with her until she fell back asleep. It took her about a half an hour.

"God only knows," I whispered to Jonathan as I got back to bed, "what they've seen and heard over there."

"She's probably just still confused," my reasonable husband said. "Like that great big Solveig said back at the Presidio, everything has happened to these kids too fast. Liana will be fine in time."

With that, he rolled over and fell asleep. I tried to do the same but my mind was racing. What might have gotten Liana into such a state?

———◉———

Well, whatever had caused the disturbance in the night, Liana was fine by the morning.

We got dressed, the two adopted girls resplendent in their new duds to the point they were smiling happily at their reflections in front of the mirror, and went downstairs for breakfast. Jonathan arranged for us all to take a bus tour of San Francisco so that we could see some of the sights before we went home the next day. It would be, I figured, another bonding experience for all of us, simply to see this beautiful city and have some fun together.

It turned out to be a jewel of a day. The sky overhead was a deep azure blue and there wasn't a cloud to be seen. The tour bus brought us past the "Seven Sisters," seven stunning Victorian buildings painted in pastel colors that were a landmark of the city. We went from there to Chinatown, where we were let out to go to a shop and where I couldn't resist getting some cute stuffed Chinese dolls for each of my girls. From there we were driven past the Haight-Ashbury neighborhood where the hippie movement had started in the 1960s. I was glad we didn't have to get out there, of all places. The last thing I wanted the children to be exposed to was anything whatsoever concerning the idea of drug-using hippies, thank you just the same. Not even as tourists. Next stop was at a park, where Jonathan took a bunch of photos of the girls and me, and after that, the tour ended at Fisherman's Wharf, just in time for us to have a late lunch there.

It was as we walked along the wharf to a restaurant that I noticed him. Again.

There was the same Asian man who I'd seen on the grounds of the Presidio the day before, the one with the drooping mustache, and the scar about an inch long on his left cheek. This time he was standing slouched by the big Fisherman's Wharf sign, which was shaped like a gigantic anchor. He wasn't wearing his sunglasses today.

I couldn't say what it was that made me wonder about him once again. He did not come across as likable, that was for certain. His eyes narrowed when he saw Jonathan and me coming along with our three kids in tow.

He could not seem to stop staring at us.

I didn't know why, but something about his gaze gave me a chill. And it wasn't even what you could call a cold day in Frisco, either.

Maybe he's never seen a family with adopted children before, I thought, trying to reason my way around how uncomfortable he was making me feel. After all, we're a family unit that doesn't look like one, and the girls in their matching blue jackets couldn't help but attract a lot of attention. Maybe dressing them alike, while a cute thing to do, hadn't really been my brightest idea.

Or maybe, I thought, my imagination was running away with me. The guy was probably just being a jerk, staring like that.

We went to lunch in a seafood restaurant where all of us had fish and chips. Bonnie and Liana had already been picking up more English words and at a rapid pace. After her first bite of the fish, Bonnie pointed to her plate and announced, "I like!"

Liana said it too, or rather, tried to. "I leak," she tried, making Holly laugh.

"You'd think she's just wet her pants," Holly said to Jonathan and me. "Like," Holly said, directing the word to Liana, to correct her pronunciation. "You say *like*."

"Lie-eek," Liana tried again.

"Close enough!" Jonathan smiled at her, and the little girl beamed. She had such a wonderful smile when she used it.

When we left the restaurant, there he was again.

That man.

The Asian one with the droopy mustache.

He was standing like a sentinel right across from the seafood place, watchful as a guard on duty. He saw us coming out the door and stared at us again.

This time I nudged Jonathan. "That guy, there," I said. "He was looking at us funny when we entered the wharf, too."

Jonathan looked at him. "Probably a Vietnamese refugee," he shrugged. "Or something. Pay him no mind."

"No, Jon, I – I really don't like his, I don't know, his attitude," I tried to explain. I was beginning to feel like Liana probably had at the table, trying to say what I meant and not quite being able to make myself clear.

"Hmmm." Jonathan looked at the man and I guess he wasn't any happier with what he saw than I was. "Let's just get a cab and go back to the hotel where we can forget about him," my husband said.

That's what we did, but when I turned back around to see the man as we walked away, I saw he was still tracking us with his eyes.

I had a feeling he had been watching the restaurant the entire time we had been inside, waiting for us to come back out.

Weirder than weird.

It made my blood run cold.

———— ◉ ————

I would have thought that after such an active day the children, or more specifically Liana, would have slept well that night.

It didn't work out that way.

Once again, the little girl let out a heck of a wail in her sleep. It was enough to wake the dead.

For the second night in a row I woke her up, and held her hand and talked to her until she fell back asleep.

"We'll be flying home tomorrow," I told her, although I knew she wouldn't understand what I was saying. "Home to Indiana. You need to get some rest because it's going to be a long day, but at the end of it, you're finally going to be home."

"Home," she repeated wearily, and then drifted back to sleep.

Chapter Six

The Bane of My Existence
December 1975

M atters were a whole lot better by Christmastime.

I had to hand it to my brother Alan and sister-in-law, Julie. When we got back to Emerson from San Francisco in April, we found they had done a stellar job of turning Liana's room into one any little girl would love. They put a child's desk in there and painted it turquoise, pink and white. They got her a Lite Bright, a Frisbee, and a Spirograph set, bought stuffed animals to arrange on her bed, and even, knowing the meaning of her original name, found a framed print of a pink lotus blossom to hang on her wall.

They were also generous enough to refuse to let us reimburse them for all they'd given our new daughter. "She's our niece," Alan said, protesting the thought of receiving any money. "We wanted to get these goodies for her." He'd also brought a Frisbee for Holly and one for Bonnie, too.

Liana seemed to love all the new toys, but pride of place in her room was occupied by the Vietnamese doll wearing the *ao dai* outfit that she had managed to bring with her all the way from the orphanage. She put that one up on a shelf on the wall, along with the new books in English that, by Christmas, she was just beginning to be able to read. Sometimes when I went into her room she would have taken the doll off the shelf and I'd find her talking to it. Initially she spoke to it in Vietnamese, but the last time I'd walked in on her having a one-sided doll conversation, she seemed to be speaking to it in English. She stopped talking to the doll and said, "Hi, Mom!"

I didn't think twice about it.

I should have, I realized later.

There had been a few bumps in the early days after the girls joined our family, but nothing that Jonathan, Holly and I felt we couldn't handle.

For one thing, Liana continued to have nights when she cried out in her sleep. Whenever I heard her, I would go into her room, sit with her, hold her hand and talk to her until she was able to fall back asleep. It started to happen less and less, especially over the summer, when the only activity the kids had was to go to arts and crafts classes in the local elementary school's summer program, swim at a nearby lake, or play outside all day. The more Liana played outside with that Frisbee she'd received from Uncle Alan, it seemed, the less upset she became in her sleep. Maybe a dose of good old midwestern summertime fun was grounding the child more in the present than the past. Thank God for that.

For another thing, and one we hadn't considered before the adoption, Emerson was a lily-white town. I had never really thought twice about it until the day after we got home from San Francisco. One of the neighborhood kids started hassling Liana and Bonnie about their Oriental looks. Both girls were gorgeous kids, so it was almost inconceivable to me that any children would mock them over their appearance, but this kid, Russell Delmonico, did, flinging all kinds of racial slurs at them, like "Chinko China Chink." The runty school age bully wasn't even swift enough to realize that *that* particular label didn't apply to Vietnamese girls and was actually a pejorative for ones from China.

That brat, Russell, lived right across the street, in spite of how often I prayed that he and his whole equally insufferable family would pack up and move. Same deal for another family that was exceedingly unlikable, the Nugents. God never heard those prayers of mine when I said them, however. Where Russell was concerned, you'd think those parents of his would have taught him to welcome the two new additions to my household to the neighborhood, but no. Such politeness was beyond the entire Delmonico tribe.

Rotten Russell, as I always thought of him, even went so far as to stretch the sides of his eyes with his fingers, in imitation of deep-set Asian eyes, stick out his tongue, and call my children "yellow-bellied sapsuckers," a reference to a type of bird that kids usually brought up in an attempt to label one another cowards. In this case, it was a slur on my new daughters' skin color.

It made my blood start to boil.

I was gardening in the front yard, heard the whole thing, and was ready to do battle with that awful boy for being so ill-bred and nasty, but my Holly beat me to it. She strode right over to Russell and threatened to sock him right in the teeth if he said one more word against her sisters. It was kind of funny to see how that brat cowered in the face of my daughter's ferocity. I had a feeling he would think twice before bothering the little ones again.

But Holly's response caused Russell's mother, Angie Delmonico, to try and start a ruckus. She was built like an apple on a stick and came charging over to my front yard after her son went home upset. "What is this I'm hearing," she asked, "that your daughter wants to knock out my son's teeth?"

"Your son," I replied, "was mocking my two adopted children. If he'd been raised by you to have some basic human decency and god manners in the first place perhaps he wouldn't have to suffer through any threats to his teeth."

Angie Delmonico stormed off in a huff. I was just glad to see that woman get her rather wide butt off my lawn.

Fortunately his insults had rolled right off Bonnie and Liana. It was their first full day in Emerson. They didn't understand the words he said yet, although surely they understood that gesture he'd made with pulling his eyes into a shape he hoped would seem Asian. It could only have hurt them, and I hoped they wouldn't face more of the same when they went to school.

Bonnie was the right age for second grade and Liana should have entered third, but the school felt it would be too hard on them, since they didn't yet speak English. The school year was nearly over by the time they arrived in April anyway. The principal, Mrs. Reynolds, put Bonnie in first grade, Liana in second.

The two of them started attending the same school as Holly and basically seemed to have adjusted to life at our Tudor-style house quite easily, and faster than I had worried they would. It was amazing how quickly they had managed to learn some basic English. Within a month of starting school they could communicate with us in broken English, maybe not perfectly yet, but well enough to hold rudimentary conversations.

After they became more fluent, I learned that the girls had both been raised as Catholics, and they fit into our family's church and traditions seamlessly.

Bonnie was like a fountain of information about her life in the orphanage. Once she could make herself understood we heard all about it, how much she had loved one of the caregivers, a lady named Loan, and how she'd had two best friends there, Cai and Ahn.

She spoke of those little girls so much that I had to wonder where Cai and An were now. Had they been on the ill-fated flight that Bonnie had initially been scheduled to go on? Were they among the dead, God forbid, or had they gotten safely to America and been adopted? Maybe I could find a way to get Marianne Bigsby from the agency to give me a little information about where they were now. If they were in the United States, it would be wonderful, I felt, to find a way to get the three girls together. What a surprise that would be for Bonnie!

Liana, on the other hand, was still guarded when it came to her past. We knew only that she came from the Star of the Sea Orphanage. I loved the name of it, but Liana didn't seem to have any feelings about the place, one way or the other. Yes, she'd been raised Catholic, she said when I asked, and yes, she'd gone to church. But that was about all we could get out of her, and it wasn't very much.

"Don't push it," Dr. Friedman, our pediatrician, had advised when I mentioned to him that Liana didn't like talking about her past. "It's probably very painful for her to recall, a child like that growing up in an institution. Not discussing it might be her way of putting it behind her as fast as possible."

I stopped asking Liana any questions after that. The last thing I wanted to do was cause her any more misery than she'd been through already.

I should have, though. I should have kept right on asking until that dear child trusted me enough to talk.

"If I didn't know better, I would swear Liana was a little British girl," Julie, who was pregnant, said to me one afternoon when she had come over for cake and coffee. "She's so stoic and has that whole 'stiff upper lip' thing going on."

Julie would know if anybody would. She was the child of diplomats who had been stationed in London during part of the years when she was growing up.

I smiled at that. "She's a Vietnamese girl originally named after a lotus blossom but with the soul of a Brit. What a unique combination!"

Liana remained a bit remote and self-contained. Whenever we were in a large group of people she seemed to scan the room, like she was checking for something. We didn't know what, but the fact that she came from a war zone where bombs had been prevalent probably had something to do with it.

Once Holly had shown Liana how to use them, she spent a lot of time in her room playing with her Spirograph set and the Lite Bright, drawing designs with one and creating pictures with light showing through colorful pegs with the other. By October she was doing very well in school, according to her teacher, and picking up a lot of concepts faster than most of her classmates.

"And your other one," Julie said, "Bonnie, she might just grow up to be a television comedienne. She's so funny."

That was certainly true. Bonnie could never just walk into a room. She seemed to make a grand entrance, bubbly and light-hearted, smiling as if she was starring in a toothpaste commercial. Once she saw one of the neighborhood girls, Gina, doing cartwheels on her front lawn she started doing them herself, and loved nothing more than doing a whole row of them from one end of our front lawn to the other. Same deal with somersaults.

She also got a big kick out of rearranging various items in our house on us, ones that we had always kept in the same place. If the television remote was usually put on the coffee table in the living room, she'd move it to a side table just to see our reaction to that. One day she moved the umbrella stand from the front door to the back. She moved my lipstick from the top of my bedroom dresser to the bathroom sink. We'd have to hunt around for our own stuff and oh, how that child would laugh. Her sparkly little laugh was contagious. Rather than getting mad at her we'd find ourselves joining in, even Liana.

Holly remained her usual gutsy self but became something of a protector, watching over her little sisters and always trying to help them get acclimated to whatever new thing was in front of them at any given moment. She was a fantastic big sister, considerate and, from what I observed, never jealous, just glad to no longer be an only child.

Their personalities couldn't have been more different, yet the three of them got along beautifully, complementing one another, I guess you could say.

In the meantime, life went sailing on. Suddenly it was December, and amazingly, or so it seemed, and the girls had already been with us for eight months. Liana hadn't had a nightmare since before

Thanksgiving, which was the biggest blessing of the season as far as I was concerned and one I was heartily thankful for. May she continue to find peace at night, I thought.

Christmas was suddenly almost upon us. Both of the girls were looking forward to Santa's upcoming visit to our house. They were as excited as Holly on the Saturday morning when we went for a ride in Jonathan's silver Chevrolet to go and purchase our Christmas tree.

The tree farm, as it was called, was a fun place. There were fairy lights strung around the area where the trees were awaiting new owners and a jolly woman was handing out free hot apple cider. The owner of the farm, Ralphie, a guy we knew from church, claimed to be one of Santa's honest-to-goodness elves, on special assignment here directed by Santa himself in his headquarters at the North Pole, and wore a pointed green hat with red trim and a jingle bell on the top to convincingly dress the part.

I remember feeling extraordinarily happy as we went along the rows of trees, trying to pick out the "perfect" one for our living room. I felt like everything I had hoped for with the adoption of these two girls had already worked out for the best and I smiled with delight as Jonathan and I trailed the girls until they settled on an eight-foot-tall blue spruce for us to bring home.

It's a funny thing, being that happy. It isn't always the best way to go. In some cultures, I'd heard, people even think that expressing too much joy tempts fate, or attracts "the evil eye." I'd never paid much attention to ideas like that, although I knew about them.

I didn't pay it any mind on that day, either.

Silly me.

Jonathan was paying Ralphie for the tree when fate must have seen me smiling too darn much and got tempted to find a way to kick me.

It came in the form of Sofia Nugent. She lived on our street, Mayfair Drive, where she pranced up and down twice a day with a dog on a leash, and was the bane of the existence of the mothers at the Emerson Elementary School PTA. Between the Nugents and the Delmonicos, I often thought that the street's name should be changed to something a lot more appropriate.

Like Grand Chaos Boulevard.

Or Troublesome Terrace.

If anybody was the bane of my existence, it was Sofia Nugent.

And, just my luck, she was heading our way.

Chapter Seven

<u>That Would Be Impossible</u>

Sofia was striding past the blinking multi-colored fairy lights over the entrance of the tree farm in a pair of red high heels and an ankle-length ostentatious mink coat. Her normally scraggly hair was done up in a disorderly French braid with an absurdly large orange silk bow at the tail end of it, something more appropriate for a child Bonnie's age than befitting a middle-aged loudmouth. As always, the way she was put together didn't come across as stylish, chic or even relatively normal. It was hard to put a finger on it, but she always looked off, somehow, like all of her pieces didn't fit together.

I mean, red high heels and a mink coat at an outdoor tree farm with dirt paths? Ridiculous!

I was standing with the girls, finishing our cups of hot apple cider, by a loudspeaker that was playing Christmas music. "Santa Claus is Coming to Town." Yet it wasn't the jolly old elf who was heading our direction.

Whenever I counted the bumps in the road that had come up after the adoption of Bonnie and Liana, Sofia and her great big mouth always made the list. She wasn't in the number one spot. She didn't bother my children directly, at least, the way Russell Delmonico did. Instead, she came down *on me* like a ton of bricks, and all because I'd adopted two beautiful children who just happened to be of another race.

The only even halfway positive aspect of that was that she didn't spew her venom all over my children. Better for her to target me than them. I could handle it. Most of the time.

I remembered what she had said when she first ran into us at the local ice cream parlor, the weekend after we'd come back from Frisco. I had taken the girls out while Jonathan stayed at home to await the plumber, who was coming to fix a problem with our kitchen sink.

"Oh, who are these children?" She'd asked sweetly, but with steel in her dark green boiled spinach eyes. "Taking some refugees out for the day, Belinda? Doing a do-gooder deed like the rest of you do-gooders do and exposing Holly to other cultures? Ha! How *quaint!*"

Quaint?

Oh God, help me, I had thought. Sofia didn't believe that outing of ours was "quaint," or even in any way positive. No, not for a minute. She was looking at the children with pure contempt, and she didn't even know the kids were mine yet.

This was another scenario I had never considered before we adopted, that there might be white adults in Emerson who had bees in their bonnets about Asians. My new children were two little girls who needed a home and Jon and I were delighted to provide one for them. Their race was a "so what" and a "who cares" to me, to Jonathan and to Holly, but a great big major problem to the wacky, prejudiced Sofia Nugents of humanity.

Maybe I should have thought of people like Sofia, and their nastiness, right from the start. After all, the great United States of America may have been made up of people who had come here from all over the world, in addition to the American Indians who had already been here, but that didn't mean the majority of whites loved the fact. In the south there had even been Jim Crow laws set up to keep the freed black slaves as far away from the white people as possible. Blacks and whites under Jim Crow couldn't even drink from the same water fountains, among a whole list of other ways those sick laws divided them, like not allowing blacks to go to the same schools as whites, or sit at lunch counters with them, or even to use the same public rest rooms. It was all ludicrous and had begun to unravel only relatively recently, in the 1950s, when the Civil Rights Movement began to fight to change it.

America had also been involved in the Vietnam War, and lots of folks had lost their sons or husbands to the conflict. More had lost fathers and grandfathers earlier, during World War Two, when we fought the Japanese. Heck, though, we'd fought the Germans and Italians in the same war in Europe, too, hadn't we? They were also the enemy at the time, but nobody here seemed to have a problem with *them*. Just with the Japanese. They didn't look like us so they were still an easy target, and there was even a belief that the whole reason America dropped an atomic bomb on Hiroshima and Nagasaki was aided by the idea that the Japanese were "not like us."

It hadn't occurred to me that anybody would ever glare at my new children over any of this, or hate them on sight because they were from Asia, either. Yet there Sofia was, doing exactly that.

God, help me, I thought again. This means You, God. Yes, You. *Do something.*

But God wasn't listening again, and Sofia was beyond divine intervention, as usual, anyway.

"These are my new daughters," I replied evenly that day. "This is Bonnie, and that's Liana. We've adopted them from Operation Babylift."

You would have thought I'd said I was holding Sofia's grandmother hostage in my garage at gunpoint from the sneer that crossed her face then. Sofia's visage wasn't really all that attractive in the first place, and how she had landed a decent husband like Howard Nugent, who was a banker, I'd never know. In addition to her strange green eyes, which always seemed lit from within with a hint of madness, she had a wide mouth like an uneven slice of cantaloupe and a nose way too big for her face. Maybe, I always couldn't help but think, if that nose of hers wasn't so huge, she might have been able to stop sticking it all over everybody else's business.

Or maybe not.

And if that thought was uncharitable of me to think, at least I didn't express it out loud to insult her with it.

She blinked, and was blessedly silent for a too-short moment. Then she blurted out, in an angry tone, "You've *got* to be kidding me, Belinda."

"And why would I do that?" I answered sweetly.

Perhaps I shouldn't have. It was better not to respond to such a creature. That only goaded her on to reply.

"You don't know, Belinda? It's the wrong thing to do, that's why. Absolutely the wrong thing. Don't you even know that much? Not *even* that much? These kids don't belong here."

"They do now," Holly piped up. "They're my sisters."

"Oh, please," Sofia said contemptuously, with a dismissive wave of her hand, as if she was swatting away a flying insect. "I've been watching all that saccharine crap about Operation Babylift on the television lately and I fully agree with those few who have the gumption to criticize it. Those children shouldn't be here, not at all, and they shouldn't be adopted into American families, either. Not at all! They belong in their own country. They should continue to be raised in their own culture, with the rest of the yellow gooks. They're not white and they never will be, and if you think adoption papers are going to change that, ha, let me tell you, they won't. I'm really surprised at you, Belinda. I always thought you were smarter than that, but I guess I was wrong."

With that astonishing statement, not waiting for a reply, she had flounced out the door of the ice cream shop.

"What," Holly said as the door slammed shut behind Sofia, "exactly is her problem?"

"Everything! There's always something with her," I replied, trying to sound casual and keep the shakiness out of my voice. "That woman looks for problems and matters to criticize and she keeps right on looking until she finds something or other to complain about. Nobody who knows her likes her."

"Yeah, with good reason," Holly nodded, then took a spoonful of her hot fudge sundae. "What did she even mean by all that? We're not trying to turn the girls white. That would be impossible."

"Of course it would," I agreed. "She's just an unhappy person, and is probably prejudiced to the core of her being, too. The female Archie Bunker of Emerson." Though that was probably unfair to the fictional television character of Archie. Even on *All in the Family*, where he mouthed off about minority groups all the time, I'd never seen him direct such a speech in front of little children. He kept his nonsense to his own living room.

The encounter with Sofia had disturbed me more than I wanted to let on to Holly, my sensible nine-year-old. At least Bonnie and Liana didn't know enough English yet to understand what Sofia had said, but her words had shocked me to the core.

All Jonathan and I had wanted to do was to provide a home for a child who didn't have one. It was a bonus that we wound up with two children instead of just one, and adoption wasn't a weird or bad thing to do. It was a kind act. Maybe Sofia couldn't see it as such because, like *The Grinch Who Stole Christmas*, my children's favorite Christmas show, her heart was three sizes too small.

I had to wonder, though, was what she had just said true? Were there really people who were *criticizing* the good intentions of the Operation Babylift adopting parents? And did they actually believe we were trying to make these Asian children into Caucasians just for giving them an American home?

It didn't make sense to me.

Holly wasn't buying it, either. "Don't look so upset, Mom. I think Sofia Nugent is just jealous of you. Her children are awful, and you've got Bonnie, Liana and me, and we're not."

"You're probably right," I had agreed. "Almost certainly right."

Even so.

Now here she was, in front of us again, at the Christmas tree farm. Her daughter, forever scowling Cecilia, who was ten and, unfortunately, in Holly's grade at school, was by her side, and her son, Jack, eleven, was off looking at the available selection of trees with her balding husband Howard. I could see Howard's shiny pate, above a fire engine red scarf, bobbing along the nearest pathway between the conifers.

"Well, well," Sofia grinned her evil grin, "if it isn't the *lovely* O'Malley family. Caucasians here, Asians there, and all with the same shanty Irish last name. Emerson's own almighty answer to the United Nations."

I seized on the snide way she'd uttered the word "lovely" and hit her back with that. "Oh, hello, Sofia. Thank you for acknowledging our loveliness," I responded in as pleasant a tone as I could manage, though I was inwardly furious, and gave her a fake smile. "Come along, children. We're almost ready to go. Ralphie the Elf and *your father* are tying the tree to the top of the car."

The tree wasn't the only thing around here that I would've liked to see tied to the top of the car. That was the sort of retaliation the likes of Sofia Nugent needed, to be tied on top of a car and driven around town for a good long time. Like an hour. At least. Scare the nastiness right out of her. If it could be eliminated from within her at all.

"Mrs. O'Malley sure is stupid," I could hear Cecilia saying, loud enough for us to hear her, behind our backs as we walked away.

I turned around at that. "You know, Sofia, you might want to stop being so nasty to everyone else once in awhile and start setting a more positive example for your children."

"Once in awhile," she replied with her trademark evil grin, "perhaps I might. Or maybe not. My children, at least, are all *mine*."

"I wouldn't brag about that," I rejoined, "if I were you. Cecilia's mouth is as bad as yours is already."

"*We* are sisters forever," Holly put her two cents in, "and that's whether you like it or not, Mrs. Nugent."

"Exactly, Holly," I nodded my approval. "Exactly!" I loved the way that kid always backed me up where Sofia Nugent was concerned.

"You should do something about your *real* kid's mouth," Sofia shot back.

"No need," I responded. "She's right."

At just that moment, the loudspeaker started playing another song. Wouldn't you know it? Just our luck, it was "White Christmas."

"That," Sofia commented grandly, with a gesture towards the loudspeaker, "is what all the rest of us are dreaming of. Having a white Christmas. All but *you*, Belinda. You are already having a *colorful* one."

"Well, we can't all be as bland as you," I shot back. "Come along, O'Malleys," I urged my children, and we turned away from Sofia as one.

With that, my daughters and I made our way to the car. I had Holly in one hand, Liana in the other, with Bonnie skipping along ahead, and tried to hold myself as tall as I possibly could as we walked away from the human viper of Mayfair Drive.

It was a short walk to the car in the parking lot. Ralphie and Jonathan had all of the doors wide open and were busy passing a rope through the back of the vehicle. They'd already secured the front of the tree and were tying down the back. Too bad they didn't batten down Sofia up there, too.

"Don't ruin the branches," Holly said to them, while I tried to stop the shaking I was doing after the latest encounter with Sofia.

"They'll survive the ride home," Jonathan told her.

"Maybe Mom won't," she added after a glance at me. "Mrs. Nugent went after us again about adopting the girls."

"Oh, *her*," Ralphie commented with a shake of his head. "That awful woman. I swear sometimes she thinks she's ten steps above God Himself."

While the girls and I were waiting for Jonathan and Ralphie to finish securing the tree, a clean-cut young man with a camera hanging around his neck approached us. It was so nice to see a guy whose hair wasn't hanging down past his shoulders, for a change. I couldn't abide the "hippie" hairstyles that still remained popular in 1975, and couldn't really understand why anyone else could, either.

"Hi," the young guy said, "I'm Wesley Lester from the *Emerson Weekly News*. You look like a nice and interesting family. Can I get a photo of all of you, including Ralphie too, in front of the car, once the tree is tied on top?"

A nice and interesting family. This struck me as high praise after what had just transpired with Sofia.

My eyes met Jonathan's. He nodded.

"That would be wonderful," I replied. Take *that*, Sofia!

Within minutes we were all smiling for the camera.

I didn't realize it, but that was another mistake.

A big one.

Perhaps the biggest one we ever made.

Chapter Eight

<u>A Christmas Surprise</u>

The *Emerson Weekly News* came out on Wednesdays, and the next issue arrived on our doorstep on Wednesday, December 24th, which happened to be Christmas Eve. At the time it felt to me like a Christmas present from the universe. We found our photo with Ralphie, with the car with the tree on top behind us, right on the front page. Every one of us was all smiles.

There was a nice article about us, too, because Wesley Lester had interviewed us after taking the picture. He, unlike Sofia Nugent, seemed to love it that we had adopted the two children from Vietnam. He told the story to his readers of how we were a Catholic family that had taken in not one but two orphans from the Babylift. He even wrote in the article that he considered what we had done to be "a great humanitarian effort."

One of the questions he'd asked us, when we gave him all of our names, was if we'd changed Bonnie's and Liana's. "Yes," I had answered without hesitation, "Bonnie was called Bihn, and Liana's name was Lien. We felt it would be easier for them to have American names, living here. Now they're Bonnie Bihn and Liana Lien O'Malley."

I should have kept my mouth shut about that. Should have just said yes, we gave them more Americanized names, period. No details. No mention of what they'd been called before.

I really just didn't know any better. Not then.

Jonathan went to the store to purchase more copies of the newspaper while I attempted to supervise the creation of gingerbread houses for each of the girls. We were making a mess of the kitchen table with frosting, gumdrops, peppermint candies, and cinnamon sticks, trying to put those houses together, but having a wonderful time. Holly's favorite Christmas record, *A Partridge Family Christmas Card*, was playing on the stereo, and we could see our beautiful tree, all lit up and glowing, through the archway that led to the living room. If Norman Rockwell could have stopped in for a visit at that moment I was sure he would have painted us.

"You would have liked *The Partridge Family*," Holly told Bonnie and Liana. "It was a great television show. It's off the air now though."

"I like *Little House on the Prairie*," Liana replied. "My favorite."

"I not like Nellie," Bonnie said, referring to the child bully on the program.

"Yeah, she's like Cecilia Nugent," Holly agreed.

I had to wonder what had been going on among the neighborhood children if Cecilia Nugent was being compared to nasty Nellie Oleson.

"I bumped into Wesley Lester at the supermarket," Jonathan reported when he came back, ten issues of the paper in a bag. I was keeping a scrapbook for each of the girls and would cut out the article to include in each of them. "He said the article about us is going to go out over the Associated Press wire."

"What that mean?" Bonnie asked. Her English wasn't perfected yet, but where that was concerned, she was getting closer every day.

"It means," Jonathan replied, picking her up off the chair and spinning her around, "that people all over the world will be seeing our pictures and reading about our family."

"Best one in town," Holly added.

Liana said nothing. She was concentrating on arranging gumdrops like shingles on the roof of her gingerbread house.

The record swung into "Rocking Around the Christmas Tree," led by David Cassidy. *The Partridge Family*, a show about a family with a band, may have no longer been on television, but that album would, I was sure, become one of our family favorites forever.

Later that afternoon, when the sun was starting to set, once the gingerbread houses were done and sitting on our dining room table as centerpieces, I found Liana standing in the living room in front of our lovely Christmas tree. The lights were out, the better to enhance the glow of little ones on our tree shine, and the windows outside were already dark, too.

The tree had turned out great. The little pink, blue, yellow, red and green lights were reflected by thick garlands of silver tinsel, making them seem even brighter than they were already. The ornaments that my late grandparents had once put on their Christmas trees were on ours now, along with ones from Jonathan's childhood and a bunch of homemade origami ones that had been created by Holly. There were wrapped peppermint sticks on the tree and brand new red, green, blue, gold and silver Christmas balls. It was magical.

Liana was holding her doll from Vietnam, the one wearing the red and white *ao dai* outfit, in her arms. "See? Tree," she was stage-whispering to the doll, this time in English. "Pretty."

"Ah, Liana, showing off the tree to your doll?" I asked her pleasantly.

Strangely, my question made her jump.

I put an arm around her. "I didn't mean to startle you, hon. Does your doll have a name? She sure is lovely."

Liana shook her head, suddenly going mute. She held the doll closer, like she was trying to protect it.

"Have you been teaching her English?" I tried again.

"Little bit," Liana told me. "I go put back." She pulled away and headed for the stairs to her room.

"You don't have to put her back on her shelf, you know," I gave it one more shot. "You can put her right here, under the tree, if you like. She might like that, being able to stay by the Christmas tree and enjoy the lights."

"No. I put doll back," Liana replied again, and went up the stairs with the doll.

Unusual, I thought. What was it about that doll? It was her one connection to her previous life, sure, and I could understand how important that was to her, but at the moment, the kid seemed to be guarding it like some kind of a sentinel. I had to wonder all over again what kind of experiences she'd had before she came here. Her English skills, like Bonnie's, were getting better by the day, it was true, but were not yet perfect, and she still wouldn't answer any questions about her life in Vietnam.

But for the moment I let it slide. After all, it was almost time to get ready to go to the Christmas Eve Anticipated Mass at our church. I was wearing my jeans and wanted to change into a nicer outfit before we left.

—————◉—————

Christmas morning was hectic and fun. Jonathan and I had gotten bicycles for each of the girls. Holly had outgrown her first small bike already so we got her a bigger one and bought bikes with training wheels on them for the other two. They woke up to find three bicycles and piles of presents under the tree, one pink, one blue, and one yellow. They got brand new parkas, winter pajamas, and games and toys galore. Holly and Bonnie were practically flying over the moon, and even Liana stopped being so stoic for a change, laughing with joy along with her sisters.

Jonathan gave me a gold and diamond tennis bracelet. I gave him a brand new set of golf clubs. What a morning!

Family came over for Christmas dinner, my brother Alan with Julie, who was now very, very pregnant, in her ninth month. Our parents drove in from Bloomington and Jonathan's widowed mother arrived from Indianapolis. All of them came bearing even more gifts for the children. Alan entered in a red and white Santa hat with a hearty, "Ho, ho ho," and a sack of gifts on his back. Ha, if his colleagues at the police department could see him now!

Jonathan's mother had a copy of an Indianapolis newspaper with her. "Look at this. You're all on the front page!" The article and picture of us at the tree farm really had gone out over the Associated Press wire.

I had known this Christmas would probably be our most memorable one of all, since it was the first one we were having as a complete family with Bonnie and Liana. Jonathan and I had been taking lots of pictures since the kids woke us up to see what Santa had brought them at five o'clock in the morning. We'd even almost run out of film. Then something happened to make the situation even more unforgettable than it was already.

We had finished a terrific dinner of turkey with all the trimmings, stuffing, carrots, potatoes, sweet potatoes, and more, and had started on dessert. There was a cake I had made with bits of crushed peppermint in the vanilla frosting, served a la mode, of course, with coffee for the adults and hot apple cider for the girls.

Julie had taken one sip of her coffee when she dropped her water, and I don't mean the drinking water on the table in her glass.

"Oh my God," she gasped, "it's time! Alan! I'm having the baby!"

"What?" Alan replied, looking startled.

"Right now?" Asked our mother.

"Can't you finish Christmas dinner first?" My dad asked, teasingly.

But Julie's pretty face contorted with pain. "I don't think," she gasped, holding her stomach, "that's going to be a possibility. My water..." She began, but winced as another rough contraction took her over.

"We've got to get you to the hospital," Jonathan said. "Right now, Julie. Come on, Alan, you help her up. We can take my car."

"You're going to have a Christmas baby!" Holly exulted. She was a Christmas season baby herself, born on December 27th. "You could name her Noelle. Or maybe Joy, like the joy of the Christmas season."

"Talk about a Christmas surprise," said my dad.

"That," said my mother, "is a fantastic idea, Holly. We should keep those Christmas theme names in the family."

Alan tried to get Julie off the dining room chair. It wasn't an easy process. She looked to be suffering quite a lot of pain.

I ran to the den, where I had stored everyone's coats, and came back with Julie's coat and purse and Alan's royal blue parka. "You'd better get a move on," I said, "or the child might arrive on our living room floor."

Julie moaned, "No!"

"Okay," Alan agreed, sliding his arms into his parka. He helped Julie into her red and black coat. "But I hope the rest of you will come by the hospital later. I'll call when the baby is here."

We finished dessert after they left, feeling a new level of excitement. My mother, who was a retired music teacher, went over to our piano and started playing Christmas carols. The rest of us sang along. "Hark the Herald Angels Sing" was followed by "Joy to the World," the hymn. Holly coaxed my mother into also playing the other "Joy to the World," the one by Three Dog Night. It was one of her favorite songs.

Liana surprised me by suggesting a song she'd learned at school. "Jingle Bells," she said with a smile. The little girl who had never seen snow or one-horse open sleighs wanted to sing a song about it.

My mother played it, and after that, she took more requests.

My parents and Jonathan's mother stayed over that night. We waited and waited to hear from the hospital but the phone didn't ring until about a quarter to midnight. "It's a girl!" Alan reported. "And she was born late on Christmas, but still on Christmas! Mother and baby are doing fine."

"Has she got a name yet?" I asked.

"We liked Holly's suggestion. The baby's name is Joy Belinda O'Malley. Her middle name is after you. Julie and I already hope she'll grow up to be as fine and generous as you are, you who gave those two girls a home."

I found I couldn't stop my happy tears.

———————◆———————

The next morning we all but invaded the hospital. All of us, Jonathan, who had returned home with Alan around two o'clock in the morning, my parents, Jonathan's mother, the three girls and me. We found Julie sitting up in bed, cradling little Joy Belinda, who was wearing a little pink outfit topped with a tiny Santa hat.

Bonnie reached her arms toward the baby. "I hold her?" She asked Julie.

"Sure, you can hold her," Julie said. "Just sit in the chair first." There was a guest chair by her bed. "Be very careful you don't drop her, Bonnie."

"I will not drop. I helped with babies a lot."

"In the orphanage?" Alan asked her.

The child nodded. "I love babies," she said.

Julie passed the baby to her and she cradled the newborn like a practiced nurse, supporting Joy's tiny head. Bonnie began singing a song to her, one she'd learned at school, rocking the newborn gently. It was the first time I'd ever heard "Jingle Bell Rock" sung like a lullaby.

"You've done this a lot," Jonathan commented, "haven't you?"

"It's fun. Helping take care of babies. Me, Ahn, Cam." Her little friends from way back when.

So they'd been like junior nursery aides. Amazing. This child had found a way to be happy even when she had been stuck in an institution. It was probably a saving grace for her.

"Better than having a doll," Holly grinned. She asked Julie, "Can I have a turn at holding her next?"

"Sure thing. But let Bonnie have her for a few more minutes." We were all impressed with the way Bonnie was taking care of baby Joy Belinda. I was glad Jonathan had brought the camera and got a photo of the moment.

"Did you help with the babies in your orphanage, too, Liana?" I asked her.

Liana looked sadly down at the floor. She shook her head.

Why, I had to wonder, does she look as though she's somehow ashamed?

Chapter Nine

Innocent Questions Without Answers
January 1976

The new year arrived a week later. All of us tried to stay up long enough to watch the ball drop in Times Square, an hour ahead of us at eleven o'clock at night, since they were on Eastern Standard Time and we were on Central, but of the three kids, only Holly managed to stay awake that long. Bonnie and Liana fell asleep on the floor in front of the television set.

It was finally 1976. This was going to be the year of our nation's bicentennial, the 200th anniversary of the founding of America. A lot of celebrations were already being planned for the Fourth of July, but I felt that was getting way ahead of ourselves. Besides, I had another idea about a possible celebration that maybe, just maybe, I would be able to pull off a little sooner, with a whole lot of luck and if all went well.

I waited another few days, until the children were back in school and couldn't overhear the phone call I wanted to make, before contacting Marianne from our adoption agency. I hadn't really talked to her in some time and she was very glad to hear how well everything was going in our family.

I told her the reason I was calling. "Bonnie – well, Binh – keeps mentioning two little girls who were her best friends in the orphanage. Cam and Ahn. From everything I've heard, I'd say the three of them had a very strong and positive friendship. I was wondering if you might have any information about them. If they were adopted to this country, who knows? Perhaps I could arrange for them to see one another."

"Cam and Ahn?" She repeated.

"Yes, Cam and Ahn."

"I think I know of the two girls that you mean. Cam I'm not sure about offhand, but Ahn went to a family from the Philadelphia area."

"Philadelphia! That's not too far away," I said excitedly. We could even drive there in about a day.

"I would have to contact Ahn's adoptive parents, of course, and see if they wouldn't mind letting you have their information, but I seem to recall they were lovely people and they'd probably be amenable to this. I'll see what I can find out about Cam's whereabouts, too."

"Wonderful, Marianne! And while I've got you on the line, I also wanted to ask, what do you know about Liana's life in the orphanage? Bonnie tells us all about her days in hers, but Liana is – is – ah, *isn't* much of a talker," I finished lamely. I didn't want to emphasize just how strange I thought that was, or that I sometimes even got the feeling that the child was actually afraid to answer our innocent questions. Her reaction with that Vietnamese doll she had on Christmas Eve had struck me as odd. Her lack of details in general was even odder.

It made no sense to me. But I hoped it might ring a few bells with Marianne.

"I would have to inquire," she replied. "I wasn't too familiar with Liana until she got to The Presidio, to tell you the truth. She wasn't in the same facility as Binh. I was more familiar with the running of that one."

"I'd appreciate it if you could find out. The pediatrician had said maybe she doesn't talk about it in order to put it behind her faster, but, you know, just in case there was anything there that I ought to know, I wanted to ask."

"I'll see what I can do. The woman, Sister Elizabeth, who ran that orphanage, Star of the Sea, lives in Los Angeles now, in a convent. I'll be sure to contact her."

With that, we exchanged a few more pleasantries and then hung up.

I loved the idea of Ahn being in Philadelphia. Bonnie would be so surprised if I managed to arrange a visit with her!

It made me wonder who Liana's best friends back there had been. Was there a child, or children, she'd been particularly close to as well? Could Marianne possibly find out about that?

I should have asked her before ending the call, I realized. But it could wait until she got back to me, and hopefully then, if she'd found out anything at all about Liana, I could always bring it up.

It was a cold and gray January day. The temperature outside was below freezing. I wondered if the former orphanage director in California, the nun, was looking out her front window, as I was, and seeing palm trees and sunshine. At least she was in the United States and reachable. Meanwhile, I thought to myself, sometimes this Indiana midwestern climate didn't always strike me as lovable.

I still hadn't heard back from Marianne Bigsby by the end of the month, but I wasn't worried. She had always come through for us before. I knew she would again. I said nothing about my conversation with her to anyone but Jonathan.

Jonathan and I, with the children in tow, of course, liked going to Catholic Mass on Saturday nights instead of on Sunday mornings, and we would meet up with Alan and Julie and baby Joy Belinda once we got there, unless of course my brother the cop happened to be on duty. The services were called "anticipated Masses" and covered our weekly Sunday obligation to attend it a few hours early. That way, on Sundays we could sleep in, then have Alan, Julie and Joy over for Sunday brunch.

The Saturday evening on the last weekend in January started out like any other. We piled into the car and rode to our church. The radio was on, and the girls were enjoying the latest hit song, which just happened to be "Saturday Night," how appropriate, by the Bay City Rollers. They were singing along and clapping to the beat at the same time. I felt a headache coming on from all the noise but didn't have the heart to silence them. We'd be at church soon enough and the girls were having fun.

It was when we got to the church that I saw him.

He had the rather gold complexion, straight black hair, and high cheekbones of an Asian guy. One cheek had a scar on it. He was wearing dark aviator sunglasses and standing right inside the church's main door.

I immediately thought that was strange. Who wore sunglasses inside of a church, of all places, in Indiana in the wintertime, yet, and especially a few minutes before a Mass at seven o'clock at night was about to start? That was the first strange thing about him, and I found it glaringly unusual.

Then there was the fact of where he had positioned himself. The temperature outside had been above forty earlier that day, sure, but now it was down into the twenties again. It was bone-chillingly cold outside. And there was a vicious wind howling as well.

Why would anybody be standing directly inside the door, in the path of the wind, if he could help it, then? Everybody else was moving away from the door as quickly as possible.

And there was one other weird feature of the guy's behavior.

Something even stranger happened.

The man was staring at Liana.

In fact, when he spotted her, he all but jumped, as if she was exactly the person he was looking for. Half a smile even touched his lips.

No, not a smile.

More like a cross between a grin and a sneer.

How could my little daughter Liana be who he was hoping to see?

But it seemed as if she was.

Liana and the other two girls were walking into the church ahead of Jonathan and me, and even when they went past him, he turned toward her, still gazing at her through his dark glasses.

Transfixed.

Liana must have sensed his eyes upon her. She looked right back at him. Pointedly, it seemed.

She also instantly became alarmed. Her eyes widened considerably and then she moved up the church aisle, fast.

Like lightning.

Almost at a trot.

Somehow or other, the man seemed vaguely familiar to me. But try as I might, at least initially, I could not place where I had seen him before. I also couldn't figure out where I might possibly have known him from. I met very few Asians in our town. Was he Vietnamese?

It will come to me, I thought to myself, and dipped my hand in the holy water font, as usual. I blessed myself, settled into our usual pew, and knelt down to pray. This was all probably nothing. There was a big Vietnamese family that had settled here during these last few months. Lots of Vietnamese had gotten to the United States as the war ended. Sometimes we saw the new family, the Trinhs, here at the church. Was it possible he was one of the Trinhs?

No, actually. I knew all of them by sight and I had not seen him with them before.

Maybe my daughter simply had reminded the guy of one of his own children or other relatives.

But I just didn't think so.

As it happened, Bonnie was sitting next to me in the pew, and Liana was next to Bonnie. I couldn't watch her too closely as the service began but I managed to glance at her from time to time. She looked a little shaken up.

It happened again after Mass was over and we were filing out the door to the tune of the organist playing the hymn, "Let There Be Peace on Earth." He had positioned himself right inside the door again, but this time he was facing the interior of the church, not looking out to see who was coming in. He was watching everyone's exodus to the parking lot.

Until he found Liana.

I made sure I walked out holding Liana by the hand and, once again, she seemed startled to see him. She jumped back a bit, let out a small cry, said a word or two in Vietnamese, and clung to my hand tighter.

Holly took her other hand, protective of her as always. "What's wrong, Liana?" She asked her, but her sister didn't answer.

"Let's get right to the car," I urged my brood to get us out the door, and away from him, whoever he was, faster. Liana all but accidentally pulled my arm out of the socket as she led the way to our car.

There is definitely something wrong here, I realized, and it's major, whatever it is. Liana's upset.

I waited until we were at home, and had a chance to discuss it with Jonathan, before we brought it up with Liana.

"I noticed him too," Jonathan said. "I couldn't make heads or tails of it, why he was looking at Liana like that. So focused on her. It was downright creepy."

"We need to talk with her. Right now, I'd say," I said.

"I agree with you. But will she tell us anything?"

"I don't know why tonight would be any different where that's concerned," I sighed with a shake of my head, "but she was scared, Jon. I'd say maybe, if she's frightened enough, we might have a shot at getting the reason why out of her."

I should have known better, though. Liana, opening up? Fat chance.

We still had to give it a try.

Of course, it didn't work.

Chapter Ten

<u>Two Bucks in a Tote Bag</u>

Bonnie and Holly were in front of the television set. Liana was sitting on the floor, with her arms around her knees, all but hugging herself. Her eyes were as close to saucers as I had ever seen them and she still looked like she was scared.

I made hot chocolate for all three of them, and poured mugs for Jonathan and myself as well. I served them to Bonnie and Holly and told Liana, "Come into the kitchen for a moment, will you, honeybunch? Your father and I want to ask you something."

Liana got up from the floor, still looking frightened. Or maybe the better word to describe her expression was wary. She took her usual spot at the kitchen table. Jon and I sat down with our mugs, I gave her hers, and tried to start the discussion.

"You have to tell us, darling," I began. "Who was that man we saw at the church?"

Liana looked at the top of the table, not at us. "Don't know." She wasn't being at all truthful.

"I think you do know," I said as gently as I could. "I'd like you to tell us."

"No matter who that was," Jonathan added, "it's going to be all right. Just let us know."

Liana's sole response was to take a sip of the hot chocolate.

"Come on, Liana," I prodded her. "We know you were afraid to see him for some reason. Now tell us. Who was he?"

This time she folded her arms and looked down at the tabletop again. She could not look us in the eye. "Not afraid of him. Don't know."

"Do you not know his name?" I asked. "Or do you not know *him?*"

Silence.

"Have you ever seen him before?" Jonathan tried.

More silence.

"Liana, this isn't good," I told her, maybe a bit more harshly than I should have, but I was upset on her behalf and wanted to know what was going on. "And it's not like you to behave like this, either. We're asking you questions and we want to hear the answers." My headache, which had started in the car on the way to the church, hadn't quite gone away yet. Now my head began to pound.

We waited.

"Can't tell you," she finally said, in a voice just above a whisper.

"You can't tell us?" Jonathan asked. He and I exchanged a look of confusion. "Why is it you can't, Liana?"

What *was* this?

Silence.

"Tell us what you mean, honeybunch," I urged.

She shook her head. "No. Can't. *Won't.*"

"Just tell us who that man was," I all but begged her.

"Not telling!"

With that declaration, she slammed both hands on the table. It made all our mugs of hot chocolate jump, hers to the point some of the liquid spilled over the side. She leapt from her seat, ran from the table, and hightailed it up the stairs to her room as though she was being chased by a whole fleet of hobgoblins. I could hear her slamming the bedroom door.

"Well, that wasn't a success," I commented to my husband.

"That child." Jonathan shook his head. "You know, right from the beginning, much as I adore that kid, I've wondered about her. It just doesn't seem natural to me for her to be as close-mouthed as she is. She's a little girl. The other two tell us everything about everything, but this one? She strikes me as having a lot of secrets. Too many of them, really, for a child who is still eight years old going on nine."

"We just don't know enough about who she is. I mean, who she was before." I rose from my seat at the table. "Come on, then. Let's follow her upstairs and see if we can get some of those secrets of hers out of her." At that point I couldn't have been more concerned. This was becoming more alarming by the second and we didn't even know exactly what *this* was.

All I knew was there was something very, very wrong going on here, and whoever that man at the church had been, he seemed to have sparked it. She had never gotten as upset as this around us before, to the point she was yelling at us and hitting the table like a diva.

The only other times that kid had ever really gotten out of control was when she'd cried out in the night. Those episodes had pretty much stopped by that point, though, and I wasn't even sure if those counted anyway, since she couldn't help it if she screamed in her sleep. Had she seen soldiers fighting in Vietnam, or experienced bombings, perhaps? And if she had, which was only a big if, and pure speculation on my part, was the sight of that Asian man enough to bring it all to the surface?

On the other hand, the way he had been studying her also was bizarre. It had seemed like he had been inside the door of that church, watching specifically *for her*.

Waiting.

For Liana.

Just waiting.

When he spotted her, it was like aha, there she was, the one he'd been looking for.

But the one *what*?

When we got up to her room, I knocked on the door and said, "Liana, it's your father and me. We're coming in."

I opened the door and was greeted by an astonishing sight.

Liana had put one arm into the sleeve of her parka and had put her winter stocking cap with the pompom on top on her head. She had also put some things into a tote bag. I recognized the cardboard box of her Spirograph set was sticking out of the top of it. The child looked like she was getting ready to flee the house.

"Liana!" I reacted in shock. "What in the world is all this?"

"Are you going somewhere?" Jonathan asked her. He tried to say it like he was only teasing, but his eyes were wide with concern.

"Going out," she replied. She struggled, with silent tears rolling down her cheeks, to get the other arm into the parka. Once that was accomplished, she hugged the tote bag closer to her. "Have to go. Now."

"But it's freezing outside," Jonathan said to her reasonably. "You're not in any trouble with us, sweetheart. You don't have to go anywhere."

"Have to," she repeated, though less strongly. She also looked from Jon to me, and suddenly seemed just a tiny bit hopeful, like maybe that wasn't going to have to happen after all.

"Do you think for one minute," I asked her, putting an arm around the frightened little girl, "that we would let you go away from us? Ever? You're our *daughter*, my darling Liana. You're Liana Lien O'Malley, and you belong right here with us."

"And there's a chocolate layer cake downstairs that's waiting for us to eat it," Jonathan added. "Aren't you hungry?"

She thought about that for a minute and repeated, "Chocolate cake?"

"There's a great big piece I've already reserved with your name on it," I decreed on the spot. "But only," I added slyly, "if you take off your coat and hat first. And unpack that bag. You're our daughter, forever and ever, and we're in the middle of a midwestern winter. You're not going out anywhere tonight."

She looked from one of us to the other, as if she were contemplating a decision. It all but tore me in two. What was going on inside of that pretty little head of hers? What was all this about? And what, exactly, had gotten her so upset?

She took off her coat and put it back on the hook behind her door, stuffing her pompom hat into the pocket. She also took the Spirograph out of the tote bag. The next item to emerge was her Vietnamese doll. She put that on the shelf by her books, where it belonged. Two one dollar bills were retrieved from the tote bag as well.

"You wouldn't have gotten very far on that," Jonathan observed drily. He was trying not to laugh.

I simply reached for my daughter and hugged her tight, then led her over to her bed and sat on it with her. Jonathan did, too.

"But before we go after that cake, you need to tell us, because this is very important, Liana," I said in as kind a tone as I could muster considering my headache had now grown to be bigger than the size of the state of Texas, or so it seemed. "Why did that man upset you? The man at church."

She looked away from me.

"Liana," I tried again. "This isn't optional, my dear. You must tell us. *Must*. Tell us. It's mandatory, okay? You know what that means? It means you can't get out of it. Have you ever seen him before?"

Liana only shrugged.

It wasn't a yes.

It wasn't a no, either.

It was an evasion.

And that was as far as she let us get on the subject of the man with the scar that night.

Chapter Eleven

<u>The Man with the Drooping Mustache</u>

We coaxed Liana into following us back down the stairs. There was a sitcom just about to start on the television and my other two were all set to watch it. I settled her on an easy chair in front of the set, brought each of the girls pieces of the cake I had made from scratch that afternoon, and went back into the kitchen to talk with Jonathan. My two adopted daughters hadn't spoken in Vietnamese to one another in the past several weeks, but they were talking in their original language now.

Holly said, "Hey, speak English!"

"*Khong,*" Liana replied, which I remembered was the Vietnamese word for "no," and went right on talking to Bonnie.

"I want to call Marianne from the adoption agency again, as soon as the girls are in school on Monday," I told Jonathan in too low of a voice for the girls to hear me in the next room. "I've been waiting patiently to hear what she's been able to find out about that child, but now I want to see if I can push her to respond faster. And I'm going to call Father Salerno tomorrow, after all of the morning church services are over. He might be able to tell us who that man was."

"Know what I'd do as well?" Jonathan asked. "I think you should pull Bonnie aside and talk with her about this. Or I could do that, if you like. The two of them have always talked to one another a lot, from the time we first picked them up in Frisco. They'd converse in their own language at first, remember that? Now they're at it again in there. Maybe Liana is confiding in Bonnie. Perhaps our littlest one will know something about whatever this is."

"I'll talk to her," I decided. "In fact, maybe what I can do is this. Tomorrow afternoon I can take Bonnie for a ride in the car and speak with her then. After that, she and I can go and see Father Salerno. But what I can't figure out is, if, let's just say *if*, that man was there to try and lay eyes on Liana, how would he have known we'd be at the church tonight?"

One of the newspaper photos of our family at the Christmas tree farm had been cut out and stuck onto our refrigerator with some magnets. Jonathan gestured to that. "Maybe," he said, "that's how."

Oh, my God.

"It went out over the Associated Press wire," I recalled in a shocked whisper.

"To newspapers all over the country," Jonathan agreed. "And the world. So did our little interview with that reporter, Wesley Lester."

"And it mentioned that we were Catholic," I added, "and living in Emerson, Indiana! If all of this isn't just some strange coincidence, Jon, if he was looking for Liana specifically, as crazy as that seems, that article gave him the means to find her."

Jonathan told me, "After the way she just reacted? I don't think that sounds crazy at all."

I wasn't surprised, that night, when Liana started screaming in her sleep again.

Jonathan and I ran into her room. She woke herself up this time and began to sob. It was heart-wrenching to listen to how much she was suffering.

But suffering from what?

The sight of that man, obviously. Yet who in the name of God was he? And what might he want with Liana?

I hated having questions without answers.

I left her with Jon for a few minutes, went downstairs, and put some milk in a pan to heat on the stove. Whoever he was, I had a sneaking suspicion that Liana not only knew him, but knew what he wanted from her, as well. She just wouldn't let us in on her secrets.

I waited for the milk to heat up, wondering about what could have happened to this dear child on the other side of the world, an open-ended question if ever there was one. Had there been some kind of abuse at her orphanage? Had she been treated harshly or with anger? Was the man, perhaps, God forbid, a pervert?

Anything was possible. From the terror in Liana's shouts and screams, not to mention the way she'd packed that tote bag and had been ready to make a run for it, I'd say anything horrific was possible.

But what could it have been?

And why would she have wanted to leave our house? That was counter-intuitive, if she was afraid of him. He was out there somewhere. She'd be safer in here.

I went back upstairs with the mug of hot milk. The child stopped crying and sipped it slowly.

"We love you, Liana," I tried a new tactic. I wouldn't ask about the man this time. "We love you. And we trust you. You're our little girl. We'd like it if you would try to trust us, too."

There. No direct questions. Just a request.

She looked from one of us to the other, as though she was trying to gauge our sincerity. She took some more milk and stunned me with her response.

"Can't," she said simply. As if it was obvious.

I could have wept.

"You can't trust us?" Jonathan repeated, the hurt evident in his voice.

She shook her head. "Told not to."

I found my voice. Now it was time for a direct question. I couldn't let what she'd just said go. "Who," I asked her gently, "told you not to trust us?"

She finished the milk. Handed the mug back to me. Laid back down on the bed and turned away from us, silently, facing the wall.

I rubbed little circles on her back, stroked her long hair. "Whoever it was," I told her, "wasn't your mother or your father. We're your parents, Liana. Children and parents trust one another. They tell each other everything. That's the way it works. There's nothing you can't talk to us about. Okay?"

No response.

Well, what did I really expect?

Jonathan and I weren't sure what else we could do except stay with her until she fell back asleep.

———⦿———

I was up early. Actually, I had hardly gotten any sleep after the disturbance Liana had made. I was worried sick about that kid, of course, but didn't know what it was, specifically, that I should have been concerned about.

Someone seemed to have told her not to trust us. Who could that have been? And why would anybody tell an orphan who got adopted not to trust her new parents in the first place? It seemed a very odd instruction for somebody to have given to an eight-year-old, to say the least.

The way she was adhering to it was also disconcerting. It seemed almost as if she didn't for one second *dare* to reveal whatever this was all about. And it was now nine months, almost ten, since she had arrived in America and joined our family.

Our little lotus blossom couldn't ever hope to fully bloom like this, I reasoned. Not when this strange unspecified something still had such a stifling hold over her, tying her up in knots that weren't, I was sure, ones of her own devising.

I went downstairs to make coffee for Jonathan and me and hot chocolate for the girls. I got the milk out of the refrigerator, the Cheerios down from the cabinet, put both on the table, set it with bowls and plates, and made some toast. My brother, his wife and the baby were coming over at eleven o'clock for brunch, as usual. It had slipped my mind completely what with everything else that had gone on.

I needed to put something or other in the oven and begin to create a nice Sunday meal, when all the while, the only thing I really wanted to do was go and see Father Salerno.

I felt it could not wait. If I had to leave my own brunch party to talk with the priest later that afternoon, I would do so. It was imperative to find out who that man was who'd caused Liana so much distress.

I chopped carrots, peeled potatoes, and cut up some steaks, putting everything into one large pot to make stew. This wasn't a day when I felt like fussing too much over the menu. I also mixed together an angel food cake from scratch and put that in the oven to bake. Easily done. Brunch and dessert. I would eat with the rest of the family while Father Salerno officiated over the last two Masses of the day, then grab Bonnie so I could question her, and go to see the priest.

Liana came down the stairs for breakfast like it was any other day. She didn't look upset, although she didn't seem particularly happy, either. She ate her Cheerios and toast without talking very much and then left the table to watch TV shows.

Jonathan, watching her go into the other room to sit before the television set, shook his head. "That one's a mystery," he said to me.

"One we've got to solve," I replied.

I don't know what brought it to mind then, but as I was drinking my coffee, I thought of our first day with Bonnie and Liana. The very first day in San Francisco when we were leaving the Presidio with them.

There had been a man outside who was standing against a tree.

An Asian man with a drooping mustache.

Then there was the second day. The bus tour we'd enjoyed. The one that had ended at Fisherman's Wharf.

Where the same Asian man with the mustache had been staring at us as we entered a restaurant, and also when we left it...

That was it!

"Jonathan," I said, "I think I know where I've seen that man from last night before!"

"Aha! Where, then?"

"Do you remember that day in San Francisco, the restaurant at Fisherman's Wharf?"

"Oh! Yes, I do. That man who was staring at us. It gave you the creeps."

"Yes, it did! Only he had a mustache then, a droopy one. I think it was the same guy, only now he's shaved off the mustache."

"Belinda, you have *got* to be kidding me!"

"I wish I was," I said earnestly, "but I'm not. "The man that day had a scar on his left cheek. So did this jerk who scared Liana half to death last night."

"She didn't notice him that day on the wharf, though, did she?"

"Not that I can recall, but everything was so new to her and Bonnie that day. She might not have been paying attention to him, thinking he was just some pedestrian in the background. Though he had been studying all of us pretty intently."

"If it's the same man, then he has a reason why he's watching us," Jonathan said slowly, working it out in his head as he spoke about it. "He must have trailed us here after that damned article came out."

"Should we call the police," I asked, "and file a report?"

Jonathan said he wasn't sure. "Eventually, if this gets any worse, we'll have to, yes, but for now, I don't know. He hasn't done anything to any of us, has he? All he did was stare at Liana last night. We can't have a man arrested for that."

"No," I agreed. "We can't. But I'm sure she knows him and that he's somehow or other got her intimidated. Jonathan, she was packing up to leave us last night. She's eight years old and wanted to go on the run."

"We need to find out who he is."

"After brunch I'll take Bonnie, go to see Father Salerno, maybe even visit that new family, the Trinhs, if he can tell me where they live. See what they might know. It's a longshot but if he's from Vietnam he might just be acquainted with them."

"And I'll work on Liana after you leave. Heck, maybe I should dangle a ten dollar bill in front of her and try to bribe what's going on out of her that way."

It was 1976, after all. Ten bucks was still a fortune in those days, especially to a child.

Chapter Twelve

<u>The Sundae</u>

I thought brunch that day would never end, but finally, around three o'clock that afternoon, it did.

"Great meal today, but you seem a bit unnerved by something," Julie observed astutely as she helped wash the dishes before she, Alan and Joy left.

"That's one way to put it." I told her the whole story, the man, the Presidio, the wharf, the church, all the way up to Liana packing a bag.

"My word," Julie gasped. "This sounds serious."

"It is. I'm on a mission to find out whatever I can about it."

"Don't hesitate," Julie advised. "And you have to talk to Alan about this. He's a detective, after all, even if in this town that means he spends most of his time chasing after teeny boppers who throw rocks or steal bicycles. He might be able to help."

Alan was watching television with Jonathan, who was holding baby Joy. I pulled my brother into the den, shut the door, and ran through the whole bizarre tale again, this time for him.

"Damn," he said, when I was done. "You can be sure I'm going to ask around about this and see what I can find out."

"Please keep me posted," Julie said to me before they left. "Do you think your children should be walking to school in the morning if this creepo is lurking around?"

"I hadn't thought of that until you mentioned it," I replied, "but good idea. I'll chauffeur them there and back until this gets resolved."

Once Julie, Alan and Joy had said their goodbyes, I went in search of Bonnie. I found her in her room, sitting cross-legged on her bed, coloring on a piece of paper with crayons.

"Hey there, Pretty Peaceful O'Malley," I grinned at her, using our favorite nickname for her, "will you come for a ride with me?"

"Okay, Mom. Where?"

"Oh, I'm not sure yet. I just need to get some fresh air. Maybe the ice cream parlor."

Bonnie sprang up from the bed. "Yes! Ice cream! We all go?"

"No, hon, just you and me this time," I told her, even though I usually I brought all of the kids out together. I tried my best never to give any one of them anything more than I gave to the others, and singling only one out for a treat was the last thing I would ever normally do.

On the other hand, this was an emergency. If Bonnie knew anything that could help us solve the mystery of Liana and that lurking man, she was the one who would likely talk, and I had no choice but to isolate her from her sisters and try to get the information out of her.

I almost felt like a cop for even conceiving of having to do this.

A bad cop, that is.

One willing to interrogate a seven-year-old and bribe her with an ice cream cone, yet.

Well, if it had to be done, and the ends might even manage to justify the means, I'd do it. I'd find a way to make it up to the other two. Or maybe, just maybe, I could make a habit of taking each child out individually every now and then, and spend time with them one-on-one. Come to think of it, that might just be a great idea.

One of which was a matter to be dealt with at some later time in the future. Right at that moment I simply grabbed Bonnie's winter coat and helped her on with it. We were out the door and into the car a few short moments later. And amen! My relief at finally escaping the house and getting that child to myself felt immense. I was under more pressure, I realized, than I had originally thought.

Well, having another child who had awakened crying and screaming in the night and wouldn't say why could do that to a mother.

I waited until we were seated at a small table in the ice cream parlor, devouring hot fudge sundaes made with mint chocolate chip ice cream and having whipped cream and big fat bright red cherries on top, before I brought up the real reason for this outing. "Bonnie, darling. Did you happen to see that man last night at church? The one who was looking at us as we went in and out?"

"Yup," she replied, spooning some whipped cream into her mouth. I think she'd picked up that particular word from watching a cartoon.

Normally I would have corrected her in as mild a tone as possible, and urged her to use "yes" instead of "yup," but not on this day. I wanted her talking, not subjected to fine-tuning.

"Had you ever seen him before?" I asked.

She shook her head and bit the cherry off the stem.

I did the same with mine. "Good, isn't it?"

This time Bonnie said, "Yes. I like this mint chocolate ice cream."

"So do I. But Bonnie, this is important. Okay? Did Liana say anything to you about that man?"

Her brown eyes met mine then. She looked a little alarmed, like she was trying to figure out whether she should answer me in the affirmative or not.

"Bonnie?" I prodded, praying to myself, dear God Almighty, if You're listening, don't let *this* child go mute on me with regard to this subject. Not now, not at this vital moment. "Bonnie, you have to tell me. Even if Liana made you promise not to say anything."

"She said he's from Saigon," she replied.

I breathed an audible sigh of relief, only then realizing I'd been holding my breath. Already we were getting somewhere.

"Do you happen to know who he is to Liana? Like, were they related, or did he maybe work at her orphanage?"

Bonnie looked at me uncomprehendingly and turned her attention back to her sundae. "Don't know. Liana not tell me that."

Of course she hadn't. She's Liana.

"Do you know why she seems to be afraid of him?"

Bonnie could only shrug. "No." She was concentrating on the sundae. "I don't think he nice."

She wasn't giving me much, but at the same time, it was something, more than I'd had before we started talking. Liana did know him, and from Saigon, her city. That much was now crystal clear, even if nothing else was yet.

"Did she, by any chance, say anything else to you about him?" I pressed her further.

"She said, 'Going away.'"

"She told *you* she was going away?" I had to clarify it.

"Yup." Her spoon went into the sundae and brought some of the mint chocolate chip ice cream and hot fudge sauce into her mouth. Then she added, without my asking, "I think he want take her back."

"Take her back?" I repeated, shocked yet again by this whole entire mess, only to have my child nod.

"Yup. I guess to orphanage."

"Did Liana say that or do you just think it?"

"I think it," Bonnie said. "My guess."

"Well, he can't take her back," I told the little girl in a confident voice, hoping to reassure her on that score. "He absolutely cannot do that. She's our child now, just like you are, and we're a family. Besides, Americans can no longer go to Vietnam, and now she is an American. None of us can go there. It isn't allowed by President Ford and the rest of our government."

"We all can't go back there?" Bonnie asked, with a smile suddenly beginning to spread across her face. She looked as if she didn't want to return to the land she had come from. Of course she wouldn't. At least, not at the moment. Here, she had a family and a home. There all she'd ever had was life in an institution.

"No, Bonnie, right now, *none of us* can go to Vietnam. Our government won't let any of our airlines fly there. Not at this point in time, after the war and the North Vietnamese takeover. One day, maybe, we can all go there for a visit, as a family, and see the sights, but if we did, we'd come right back here after the trip was over. *This* is our home. Right here in Emerson, Indiana."

I dug in and ate some more of my sundae, blessing the loquaciousness of this spectacular child, and processing how this new information changed matters considerably. Now I felt certain that Liana hadn't been trying to run away from us last night. She had simply been trying to escape the clutches of the man who wanted to return her to her original homeland. But why would she believe that was what he'd come to Emerson for in the first place?

But wait. Was Bonnie's wild guess really even what was actually going on here? If she didn't know for sure then there was no way that I could figure this out yet, either. Liana, typically, hadn't told her everything.

I was getting ahead of myself there. "Would you know," I asked Bonnie now, *"anything* the man told her?"

Bonnie nodded. "Yes. She in trouble if she not do what he wants."

That line made my blood curdle. Dear God! "What is it," I asked, feeling a shiver run down my spine as I did so, "that he wants?"

"Her to do, like, mission," Bonnie replied. She must have picked that term up from a spy program that was often re-run on the television. "In Saigon, he give her secret mission."

A secret mission? Now that definitely was a line that came from the TV. It nevertheless shocked me straight to the core.

"What? She's supposed to complete a mission?" I repeated, outraged at the very thought of an eight-year-old even having one. "Is that what you mean?"

Bonnie gave a nod and shoveled more of the sundae into her mouth.

Maybe I was starting to sound like an Alpine echo, repeating this, and repeating that, but by God, this situation, which was already crazy, was quickly flying right over the line to the point it was becoming insane. "What the hell is her *mission?*"

Bonnie was about to reply when a figure suddenly came through the door, blocking some of the light.

For a second there I was afraid it was the man, but it wasn't.

It was, perhaps, the only creature I didn't want to see coming, in addition to that wretched man.

Sofia Nugent, with her hair all askew as usual.

Along with both of her rotten children. Cecilia and Jack came right through the entrance behind her.

"Can we keep one of the puppies when Queenie finally has them?" Cecilia was asking.

"Maybe just one," Sofia was saying. "We can make a pretty penny selling the rest. Queenie met up with Mr. Arnold's dog so they're going to be pure Cocker Spaniels, not mutts, and therefore they'll be worth something."

"We should keep two," Jack insisted, "one for me, and one for Cecilia."

That's when Cecilia spotted Bonnie and me and gave a nudge to her mother. "Look who's here, Ma."

"Well, well! If it isn't Belinda and her little Viet Cong communist daughter," Sofia smirked, referring to the North Vietnamese army. The enemies of America and South Vietnam. What a thing to say about Bonnie! Both of my children came from Saigon orphanages and Saigon was in the South.

Sofia surely knew that and used the "Viet Cong" reference deliberately, knowing it was wrong, simply to insult us.

"You'll say anything to try to feel superior, won't you, Sofia? My children weren't in any way associated with the Viet Cong," I informed her, as her son laughed in my face and her daughter pulled at her eyes to make them look slanted while also sticking her tongue out and crossing her eyes at Bonnie.

So low-class. All three of them.

"Oh, really?" Sofia challenged, raising a badly overly penciled eyebrow in my direction. "How would someone *like you* ever be able to tell who your children are, or what side they were on over there?"

Sofia didn't wait for a reply. She just cackled and stomped, without trying to, in her red high heels over to the counter, along with the brats, to place their orders.

My hands balled themselves into fists, involuntarily.

I could never stand Sofia. She was always monstrous, and to everybody. It probably wasn't even as personal as she always tried to make it. She was just unpleasant to the core and forever hell-bent on putting everyone around her down in order to build herself up. The put-downs never failed to be vicious, but I doubted she ever managed to make herself feel better from saying them because they never seemed to stop.

The ridiculous witch had recently caused a ruckus at the last PTA meeting over the school book fair, trying to wrest control of it away from Lara Silverstein, the PTA President, who had done a terrific job with the event for the past five years.

In all probability, Sofia didn't even truly want to run the fair herself, no matter what she said about it. She just wanted to ruin Lara's chances of having another successful event. In the twisted mind of Sofia Nugent, somehow or other, and it was hard to figure out precisely how, if Lara did a good job of it again, that would show Sofia up. The entire world, at least to Sofia, seemed to be one big, giant-sized, endless competition against her, and she was forever trying to win it.

Forget her, I told myself. You're not here to do battle with Sofia Nugent. She's like a cross between a snake and a demon and on top of that she's not rational.

It was a lot more important to get Bonnie back on the track of Liana and that horrible man, and to return our discussion to this incredible idea the child had just been relaying, before we were so rudely interrupted. That Liana had been assigned to complete *a mission*, as incomprehensible as that might seem, even as a vague thought, let alone a reality.

Yet I had heard of stories that some of our soldiers had returned home from Vietnam telling the rest of us. Even my own husband, who had been in the Air Force, came back with some harrowing stories of treachery and double-dealing among the Vietnamese population. Sad but true. Their war had been a civil war, first and foremost, before America ever got in the middle of it.

There were first-hand accounts of how you could never know, over there, whose side anybody was on.

How you could be friends with somebody Vietnamese during the day, thinking they were one hundred percent on the side of the South Vietnamese cause, and then find out later that secretly, at night, that buddy of yours was really a spy for the North, the Viet Cong.

How sometimes, a child could be coming along the street, carrying a package, or even a baby, and if the parcel or the baby was handed to an American, or to someone South Vietnamese, it would turn out to be attached to a bomb, an honest-to-goodness wired and ready to explode incendiary device, and *BOOM!* The child, or the baby, or the parcel, and the target, all three, would be blow up.

It was beyond me. I could not fathom for one second, whether a war had been going on or not, what kind of a monster would use children and babies to set off explosives.

But some of them had.

And if there were those over there who had perpetrated that, what kind of a "mission" had my Liana been charged with completing over here?

"Bonnie," I tried again now, "did Liana tell you what this, ahem, *mission* of hers was?"

Across the room at the counter, Sofia was saying to her children, too loudly, of course, in order to make absolutely sure we heard her,

"Unlike certain *other* people, I'm raising you two to always stay with your own kind and do the *white* thing."

"Not the *yellow* thing, right, Mom?" Cecilia asked, with enough volume to be heard by the last row in the balcony if this had been a grand scale theater.

But it wasn't. It was a tiny ice cream shop with only half a dozen tables and her voice reverberated along the walls.

"Precisely!" Sofia, cackling her shrill, nasty laugh, sat down at a table right next to ours, carrying a little cup of pink ice cream. Her wretched children joined her. Again she spoke deliberately with blaring decibels, enough to give me another headache. "Here's a history lesson for you, kids! Did you know there was a popular saying during the Vietnam war when it was hard for our soldiers over there to tell whose side people were on, North or South? So you know what they used to say? 'Kill them all – let God sort them out!'"

That made little Bonnie jump in her seat, quite startled. Of all the English phrases she still didn't know yet, for some reason she understood that one.

Maybe the child had heard it over there.

And how strange was it that Sofia would say such a thing just exactly as I'd remembered those stories of kids being used to carry bombs over there? The whole chaos with the treachery that sometimes arose in Vietnam over figuring out who was who.

But God almighty! She's laughing about a saying like *kill them all?* Sofia never stopped being beyond ridiculous.

All of a sudden I just couldn't stand it any longer.

I also couldn't help myself.

I rose from my seat.

I had my half-eaten hot fudge sundae well in hand.

It was time to fight back.

To get even.

For once. And for all.

Against Sofia.

And I dumped that hot fudge sundae right on top of Sofia's nasty little head!

"Why don't we let God sort *that* out, Sofia?" I asked her with my sweetest smile.

Sofia began yelling and screaming to the store owner, "Call the police! Call the police! I've been assaulted with a sundae!"

Bonnie couldn't stop laughing.

Neither could I. Assaulted *with a sundae?*

Jack and Cecilia began calling me every name in the book, and quite a few more I'd never previously heard, using lots of ingenious combinations with a certain F word, in addition to speculations about my origins, which they proclaimed involved my mother and a goat.

"Finally," I ignored them and noted to Sofia, whose unruly hair was now dripping with green ice cream, chocolate chips, and a heavy amount of whipped cream besides, "finally, finally, finally, your hair is an improvement!"

"Call the goddamn police," Sofia roared again.

The owner of the ice cream shop, a hefty older man, was too busy laughing out loud and shaking his head to comply with that.

I gathered up my coat and purse, told Bonnie to grab her sundae and coat, took the little one by the hand, and we hightailed it back outside before the Nugents could retaliate with a full-on food fight, all the while wondering if I might find myself forever banned from the ice cream shop.

If so, it was worth it!

Chapter Thirteen

<u>Grandma Trinh</u>

Bonnie and I escaped from the ice cream parlor without any flashing lights, sirens, or cops following behind us to arrest me for my, ahem, "assault." I knew Sofia would try to get back at me somehow, but for the moment, for just this once, I got *her*, and that little fact made *this* into one very satisfying afternoon.

It was on to the rectory of the church to see if Father Salerno could spare me a few minutes.

He was there and even answered the rectory bell himself. "Belinda and Bonnie! Come on in," he greeted us jovially. He was a thin dark-haired man with a ready smile and directed us into his office. "What can I do for the two of you today?"

I wasn't sure if I should let Bonnie listen to what I wanted to ask him or not, so I said, "Could my little girl wait outside the door for a minute while we talk?"

"Of course," he agreed. But first, he opened his desk drawer and gave Bonnie a lollipop.

"I'll be right out, sweetheart," I told her, and left her sitting on a bench underneath a crucifix.

One inside the office with the door closed I got right down to business, explaining about the strange man we'd seen at the church the evening before, the one in the sunglasses with the scar on his face who we believed was Vietnamese. Did the priest know who he was?

"No," he replied, dashing my hopes of getting the guy's name, "but I did see him last night now that you mention it. He was sitting a few rows back from you, where you usually sit on the left side of the church. I couldn't quite figure out why he had those sunglasses on, but to each his own, right? He sat on the aisle, and I noticed, from the pulpit, that he was paying more attention to people on the left side of the church than to me and my sermon." He laughed. "A lot of people don't pay attention, so that wasn't anything really unusual, but he did seem to be riveted in the direction of where you and yours were sitting. Why, Belinda? Was there a problem?"

"Was there ever." I gave him a brief rundown of how frightened Liana had been of the man, and what Bonnie had just told me concerning the whole outrageous idea that, before Liana ever came to this country, there was a task of some sort that he had charged the child with performing.

The good father gave a low whistle. "This is eerie," he said to me. "A *task?*"

"Yes. It's got my mind blown. My child was about to run away from home last night over it. We even caught her packing a bag, Father. Later she woke up in the middle of the night, screaming again, and that hasn't happened since she first came to us. I don't know what's going on yet. It's a ghastly mystery. But, Father, I also have another question for you. Do you know where that new family from Vietnam is living at the moment? The Trinhs?"

"Yes, I sure do. They live in an apartment right over the hardware store on Main Street."

"I'm thinking maybe, just maybe, they might know who he is, this man who has Liana in an uproar."

"Perhaps. They are, as far as I know, the only Vietnamese people in town, in addition to your two daughters."

"I'm going to go from here to see them, and maybe they'll be able to shed some light on this."

He wrote their exact address down for me on a piece of paper. "Here, take this. And let me know what happens. I'll be praying for your little Liana."

"Thank you, Father Salerno." With that, I collected Bonnie from the waiting area and we left.

"Where we go to now?" She asked.

"We're going," I explained, "to visit that Vietnamese family that just moved here. The Trinhs."

Bonnie said, "Phuong Thi Trinh's in my class. At school."

"Really? You should have told me sooner. Phuong, is that a girl or a boy?" I had never heard the name before.

"Phuong is a girl."

"Well that's great! You two can be buddies! We'll have to have Phuong over to play with you and Liana and Holly."

Bonnie grinned. "Teacher say same thing."

"The teacher *said* the same thing," I said, "that's how you say it, darling."

"The teacher said the same thing. Okay, Mommy?"

"Perfect."

We drove from the church over to Main Street. The Trinhs were at home. I was surprised when they opened the door to their small apartment to see how many of them were living there. I counted seven children, a mother, a father, and what looked like three grandparents. The place was overcrowded, to be sure, and yet everything still looked as neat as a pin. The entire family, apparently, had recently managed to emigrate from Vietnam, and since they'd only just arrived in Emerson, I had to wonder how they'd managed to get away from there.

A little girl, obviously Phuong, ran to greet Bonnie with wide open arms, thrilled that her little friend had come by to visit. The mother, Hua, seemed just as happy over it. Right away she asked me to sit at her table and poured me some tea. Some of the other kids looked on a bit enviously as Phuong and Bonnie started to play with a checkers set. Perhaps they hadn't made any new friends yet.

The father, whose name was Bao, spoke the best English of any of them, he said, so he joined Hua and me at the table. His wife Hua turned out to be pretty fluent herself.

They began telling me their story. The Trinhs had been among the "Vietnamese boat people." They'd left their country illegally on a rickety boat that sailed the ocean for over a week until they reached Thailand.

"The deck of the boat was crowded with people," Bao related, "hundreds of them, and we were outside, on the deck, the whole trip. You could barely lie down at night. People took turns sleeping. Worst of all, there were storms at sea."

"Scary," said Hua, shivering at the memory.

"The storms were the worst of it," Bao went on. "It was bad enough to be on that deck day and night to begin with, but then there was the wind, the rain, and the biggest waves I have ever seen. Thunder and lightning. It was in August that we left. A terrifying trip. The camp in Thailand where we ended up for a few months was like being in paradise in comparison."

"Paradise in a tent," laughed Hua.

"But we made it," Bao said with a smile. "All of us. All but Hua's father who had died before we left, at the end of the war. We got out as a family, intact."

"And thank God you did," I said.

"God is good," said Hua.

I was fascinated by their story, and not only by what they'd been through but what it meant. For an entire extended family to have risked their lives on the deck of a boat in the open seas to get to a country where they could experience freedom was an act of courage in the face of desperation. The communist takeover must have been pretty bad for these nice people to have done what they did to get out of there.

Finally, after about an hour and three cups of tea, I asked about the man with the scar. Had they seen him anywhere near the church?

Hua said no.

Bao also said no, but then he went into their crowded living room to consult with the rest of the family.

One of the grandmothers, amazingly, said yes. She had seen a man fitting that exact description, one with a scar on his left cheek. He had addressed her on the street when she was coming out of the grocery store after purchasing some items for dinner. It had happened two days earlier. He spoke to her in their own language, she said, through Bao who was acting as the translator.

But he wasn't from South Vietnam, she added. She could tell that much. His accent, and his use of several different words, was enough to let her know he came from the North.

A lot of the North Vietnamese lexicon was different, but she was able to understand him. He was looking for a very young girl. Not this one, the grandmother said, gesturing toward Bonnie, but another. He showed her a newspaper clipping of the child.

I had hung my shoulder bag on the back of the kitchen chair where I was sitting and dug out my wallet, where I kept several photographs of all three of my children. "Is this the one?" I asked her, holding out a photo of Liana.

Yes, she said to Bao, adding that the man had said the girl's name was Lien.

She didn't like the look of him, she continued, through Bao. She didn't like the idea that there before her was a Vietnamese man who sounded like he came from the North, either. What was he doing here? How had he managed to get to America? The North Vietnamese were no fans of the Americans. Basically she thought it didn't add up.

Grandma Trinh didn't like any of it.

I said to Bao, "Can you ask her if he told her who he was to the child? Lien, we call her Liana now, she's my other adopted daughter, and something about this man has her terrified."

Bao translated.

The grandmother replied, in Vietnamese, and Bao translated her words back to me again.

"She said," he told me solemnly, "that the child Lien was his niece."

"His *niece?*" Jonathan repeated after Bonnie and I returned home later that night. We were in our bedroom with the door shut, the better to discuss everything out of the children's earshot.

"I don't know if I buy that part of his story at all," I had to say. "Phuong's grandmother said he had a North Vietnamese way of speaking. Liana's from the South."

"That doesn't mean she *isn't* his niece," my rational husband said. "Just like with our civil war here, when our North fought the South, there were families that got separated, with some members on one side of the Mason-Dixon line and other ones on the other."

"I get all that," I said, "but still, I have to wonder. It's pretty *convenient* for him to claim she's a relative, especially if she really isn't, wouldn't you say?"

"You're right," Jonathan admitted. "It is."

"So maybe she isn't. That's what I'm hoping. I mean, saying she's related gives him an excuse to be looking for her. When we asked Liana if he was related to her she only shrugged."

"Well, that's pretty much her answer to just about everything," Jonathan commented, throwing his hands up in frustration. "She shrugs, or she says she doesn't know."

"I should think she would know if he was her uncle. And from the bad vibes he gives off, not to mention the way he frightens her, I have to say, I hope to God Almighty Himself that he isn't. Oh, and there's more."

I told him about what Bonnie had said, that he wanted Liana to perform some kind of a mission.

My husband thought about it for a few moments. "You know, that's insane, but that just might be it."

"What might?"

"That he's got some kind of plans for her. But what could he possibly be thinking of having her do? This year she's only in the third grade!"

I shook my head, not knowing what to say, really. "You know, I think of all those stories I've heard. Servicemen coming back from Vietnam, talking about how sometimes the Viet Cong used children, innocent children, to carry bombs and all that."

"Cruel as hell, that. Yes. Sick! But I fail to see why he'd want *our daughter* to be running around with a bomb here in Emerson. During wartime, actions like that are horrific, sure, but war's a whole other matter. But here? What would be the point?"

"No idea whatsoever," I admitted.

"It's got," Jon said, "to be something else."

"Well thank God for that much!"

And that was where we left it, for lack of any better ideas.

Chapter Fourteen

<u>A Last-Minute Orphan</u>

It wasn't until I was lying in bed that night that I realized I had never managed, back at the ice cream parlor, to get Bonnie to tell me what kind of an action that man who was after Liana expected her to take. Leave it to Sofia Nugent to have interrupted our discussion at just the most vital possible moment. After that, Sofia's snide remarks, and my divine little chance at taking some nice, long overdue, hot fudge retaliation, had gotten in the way of continuing questioning Bonnie.

I would have to take her aside again today, after school.

That was my initial plan, anyway.

The next day I drove my children to the school, telling them it was too cold outside these days for them to be walking.

"You never drove me to school in the wintertime before," my astute little Holly pointed out.

She was right. I hadn't, but I let it slide. The school was only seven blocks away and Indiana kids were used to cold weather. "Well, I'm driving now. I'll be back at the school to pick you up at three o'clock. Don't walk home. Okay? Do *not* walk home. Wait out front, by the main entrance. Not the side entrance, okay? The main one. When you come outside look for me and my car."

Yet once we arrived at the school, I told Liana and Bonnie to go ahead in but asked Holly to wait.

"I'm going to be late if you make me wait, Mom."

"No you're not. You can get right inside in a few seconds. I just want to tell you that if you see that man from church anywhere, the one who scared Liana, you have to let me and Daddy know. You need to let Uncle Alan know, too. Okay?"

"Okay. But who is he?"

"Daddy and I haven't figured that out yet. It might turn out to be nothing. But until we're sure, we want to be careful, okay? We really don't like the way he upset Liana."

"Okay. I don't like how he made her feel either. Now will you let me go in?"

"Of course! Get a move on, kid." I gave her a high five and she hightailed it out of the car.

My car, unlike Jonathan's gold Chevrolet Caprice, was a rather hard one to miss. It was a light turquoise blue Ford Falcon that I'd had since 1969 and its roof was usually the highest one in any parking lot. That car was so out of style now that it was well on the way to being considered a modified jalopy at this point. I'd always had used cars before Jonathan surprised me with this one for Christmas back in '69, when it was spanking new and in my favorite color. I could have gotten a new car but just didn't have the heart to give that Falcon up.

I wondered if I should tell the school principal, Mrs. Reynolds, or Liana's teacher, that there was a guy lurking around the town who seemed to have a creepy interest in the child. Maybe this afternoon, when I returned to pick them up, I would go into the principal's office and mention it, I thought. Perhaps by then I'll know more, after I reach Marianne from the adoption agency.

The minute I returned home I called her. She picked her phone up after only one ring and was in a chattery mood.

"Belinda O'Malley! I've been meaning to call you and meaning to call you about Bonnie's friends from the orphanage. Sorry I haven't. I had to attend my uncle's funeral last week out of state and things have been crazy. But I found them both. As I told you, Ahn's living with a family in Philly and I have their address and phone number for you to contact them. Ahn's called Annette now, Annette Sheridan. As for Cai, she's living in a town near Seattle. Her parents also don't mind if you get in touch. These days she's called Katie DeVries."

"This is wonderful news," I said, when I could get a word in edgewise, that is, and I meant it. I'd almost forgotten, with all the chaos regarding Liana, how much I had wished I could arrange a surprise Bonnie with a visit from her two long-lost friends. They weren't going to be lost to her any longer.

"But Marianne?" I added. "Something's come up with Liana recently, and I really need to know if you were able to find out anything about her. About her past, or if she had any relatives, or, well, really, anything, whatever you might know."

"Is there a problem?"

"Is there ever!" I went into the entire story, the night screams, the weird man, his claim of being her uncle, and all of it.

"I wish I could help you," Marianne finally said, when I had finished. "But the truth of the matter is that when I checked with the director of her orphanage, Sister Elizabeth, the girl had not been there for long before it was evacuated. She was one of those last-minute orphans."

"What," I had to ask, "is a last-minute orphan?"

"One of those children who was dropped on the steps of an orphanage right before Saigon finally fell to the North Vietnamese," Marianne replied. "There was a lot of that going on at the very end. Mothers, especially ones where the children had American, were desperate to get their children out of the country, afraid there might be reprisals against their whole families."

"What! Reprisals?"

"Crazy, isn't it? But yes. Consorting with the enemy and all that. They were bringing the kids to places like the Star of the Sea Orphanage, especially if rumor had it that the place was going to be evacuated and the children there were going to get out through Operation Babylift. Lien appeared to be fully Vietnamese, but she showed up right at the end, before the fall, too. Of course, some other parents, South Vietnamese loyalists, just wanted to get their children away to freedom, and a few of those were deliberately abandoned, too."

I couldn't imagine it. If my country were invaded I would never have given my children up, no matter who was taking it over. But I was here, not there, so what did I know? "Do you think she had a mother or a father who brought her to the orphanage, Marianne?"

"Nobody knows how she came to be there, Belinda. Sister Elizabeth said Lien wouldn't say when she was asked. All we know is that from her condition when she was found, I can tell you, it's doubtful she had well-off, concerned parents who were on a roll to get her evacuated out of the country by any means possible. What I can tell you is that your daughter Liana wasn't even there at Star of the Sea for a full week when she was sent to America, to San Francisco, to your husband and you, on an airplane."

I could hardly believe this. The whole idea of what Marianne was saying suddenly hit me like a punch to the gut. A really hard one. No wonder the girl didn't like to answer questions about her orphanage! She hadn't been there long at all.

Was Liana really an orphan, then, a child without parents?

Or wasn't she?

Might she even have a mother and a father back in her home country who were missing her and regretting what they had done in giving her up?

Was that man who had upset her really her uncle, or even her father?

"What little we do know," Marianne went on, "was that when Lien arrived at the orphanage, she was hungry and thirsty. She was wearing dirty clothes, but she was also carrying an expensive-looking doll. That wasn't the way the kids from intact families, with parents who wanted to get them out, usually came to be there. The director thought it was odd. Everything was a total mess at that point, the city was about to fall, and people all over town were going halfway berserk, trying to find a way to emigrate, pronto. A lot of the Vietnamese married foreign nationals they hardly knew, in a rush, just to be able to get out of there, to get visas for other countries that would give them citizenship once they were part of a married couple. People were all over the airport, on the roofs of the buildings, even on the tarmac, hoping to get out on planes. The embassies that were still open were flooded with potential emigrants. It was a madhouse."

"I remember some of the scenes on the television news," I said. "It was like a riveting horror story."

"Even so, getting back to Lien, since the child was unkempt and hungry, that doll she had with her was one she could have sold for food money. But it wasn't. The little girl even, apparently, brought it with her on the plane when she was finally evacuated."

"She did," I confirmed. "She keeps it upstairs in her room." Like a treasure, I thought to myself.

"The only other thing that the Sister Elizabeth remembered," Marianne went on, "was that when she asked your daughter for her address, Lien said she didn't have one any longer. She mentioned she'd been living on the street."

"On what street?" I asked naively, not initially being able to wrap my head around that.

"On *the* street," Marianne clarified. "That was Lien's story. She was a little street urchin. She said she had lived with her mother, but then the day came when her mother was suddenly gone. Lien didn't know what happened. Her mother disappeared, or was killed, maybe. Or, those days, perhaps it might even be more likely that her mother found a way to flee from Saigon, an opportunity presented itself, and she simply left Lien behind. It's all pure speculation because the child didn't have any clue where her mother had gone, or why. Anyway, after that happened, Lien claimed she wasn't allowed to stay in their apartment any longer, and said she had been sleeping wherever she could, like in parks or doorways."

"In *doorways!*"

"Yes. Sad but true. She wasn't sure for how long that went on. The director believed her story, and normally would have questioned such a child a lot further, but she didn't have time to dwell on it right at that moment. She had an orphanage to evacuate. So how Lien came to be at the Star of the Sea Orphanage was a mystery then, and it's a mystery yet. The director believed that maybe some good Samaritan had found her and had the decency to rush her over to the orphanage, where at least she would have gotten off the street and had some shelter, a roof over her head. Beyond that, we simply don't know."

"Do you know," I had to ask, "if Liana had an uncle?"

"An uncle? I don't think so. But I can call Sister Elizabeth back a little later and try to find out. It's still too early for me to call her on the phone. She's in California."

"I would really appreciate it if you would."

"You'll hear from me in a few hours, if I can reach her."

I asked for the phone numbers and addresses of Ahn and Cai's parents. Ahn and Cai, who were now Annette and Katie. It was anybody's guess what *their* stories had been like. At least they were both alive, hadn't died in that horrible crash, and had new families that wanted them.

I hung up the phone, highly disturbed at everything I had just heard.

Liana, my sweet little girl, age eight, had spent time living on the streets of Saigon during a war.

It was pathetic. Horrifying.

Dangerous, too. Any one of the wrong kind of people, make that the wrong sort of *men*, could have found her out there when she was all alone and harmed her.

As backgrounds go, hers couldn't have been worse.

My little Liana Lien O'Malley was damned lucky to be alive.

But why, if she had had no problem revealing all of this to the orphanage director, couldn't she have told me at least a little bit about it?

It was so frustrating. The only one who really knew the whole story of what Liana had been through over there in Vietnam was *Liana*, and discussing it with Jonathan or me didn't seem to be an option for her.

Which brought to mind the same old question.

Why?

Chapter Fifteen

<u>Retaliation</u>

I waited for the phone to ring, for Marianne to call me back, and puttered around the house. Or rather, I made an attempt at it, despite trying to digest everything she'd already told me, which wasn't easy, to say the least. I tried to perform little boring household tasks just to keep busy anyway. I was upset to the point I felt jittery, like I was bouncing off the walls on the inside, even though I wasn't on the outside.

I polished the silver tea set that had been given to me when I got married, the one that was mostly decorative, that sat on my dining room hutch, but that I rarely ever used.

Strange. I've got a beautiful silver tea set. But I almost never utilize it. I've got a nice Tudor-style house, a great husband, and all the good things that money can buy.

Meanwhile my child had had no choice but to live homeless, sleeping in Saigon doorways or parks or who knew where else, after her mother left her and she wasn't allowed to stay in their apartment.

My child went through that.

How could this be?

What kind of a world were we living in where someone would evict an eight-year-old girl and just leave her to fate and the elements?

That made me wonder about this "good Samaritan" Marianne mentioned, the one she thought "probably" got Liana to the orphanage. Obviously it wasn't the landlord of the building where Liana and her mother had lived. If that particular jerk had had any humanity on any level at all, she wouldn't have been on the street in the first place.

Whoever that landlord was, he or she should have personally taken Liana to an orphanage, to safety. Or maybe should have called a social worker or a policeman to do the honors. Anything except tossing my little girl out and leaving her to fend for herself!

I sighed, wondering how miserable, and hungry Liana must have been in those days. Well, we could provide her with plenty to eat now, and plenty of treats as well. Nice clothes and peaceful days. With all of that in mind, I made two more trays of chocolate chip cookies for the girls, knowing she loved them.

After that, I was about to get out the cake mix box and start creating a cake for that night's dessert when the phone rang. At last! I made a flying leap to grab it, but it wasn't Marianne.

It was Lara Silverstein. President of the Emerson Elementary School PTA and one of my best friends.

She was giggling like she was Holly's age. "How did you do it?" Lara asked me without any preamble.

"Do what?" I asked.

"Commit an assault on Sofia Nugent with a deadly bowl of ice cream?"

I started to laugh, too. "Oh, that! Well, what can I say? She was being her usual charming and delightful self, and, I don't know, let's just say *the spirit of righteousness* just *moved me* to hit her with it."

"I would have *paid* to see that!"

"She was worse than ever yesterday. I'd say she even beat her own record of nastiness, accusing little Bonnie of being Viet Cong."

"What! That's awful! No wonder you dumped ice cream on her head! So sorry I missed it."

"Maybe we could arrange to have a repeat performance and then you can witness it."

"She'll give you another opportunity, I'm sure. Maybe I'll bring a can of whipped cream to the next PTA meeting and the minute she starts up I'll squirt some of it at her."

"Maybe," I got into the fun and said, "every single one of us who are in the PTA should come equipped with cans of whipped cream, and we could all get her with them in unison."

"You do know she's carrying on about you all over town, Belinda."

"Good! If I ever go back to work, I'm going enter hitting Sofia Nugent with a sundae on my resume under the heading of official accomplishments."

"You deserve a medal for it. Will you be at our meeting later on this week?"

"I'll probably have to go in there wearing armor, if Sofia is coming, but hey, of course I'll be there. I wouldn't miss it."

<hr />

The next call came after lunchtime, just as I put the cake in the oven. This one wasn't from Marianne, either.

It was from Mrs. Reynolds, the school principal.

Holly had been injured at school with what appeared to be a broken arm.

"She what! How in the world did *that* happen?" I asked.

If I had been on edge before, my nerves were practically shot now.

"She was attacked in the gym, I'm afraid," Mrs. Reynolds reported apologetically, "at lunchtime, when we let the kids play in there after they ate in their classrooms, since it's too cold for them to run around outside today."

"Who attacked her?" I demanded.

"The Nugent kids, Cecilia and Jack. They ganged up on her. I'm so sorry about it. I'll be expelling them both for a few days. From what I've been able to gather, it had something to do with an ice cream parlor incident, but I haven't been able to find out what."

"Good God almighty! I'll be right over there to pick Holly up and bring her home."

"You'd better bring her straight to her pediatrician," Mrs. Reynolds said firmly, "not home. It looks to me like a pretty bad break."

"The pediatrician. Yes, of course, that's what I meant." I was getting so upset about Holly's situation that I could barely think straight.

I was no longer laughing about the shenanigans at the ice cream parlor now. I should have known, damn it! I definitely should have *known better* than to let myself get carried away over anything so asinine as the latest blast of rudeness and prejudice that had come out of the mouth of Sofia Nugent.

Of course her children had made it a point to get even with one of mine for what I had done.

Of *course* they had!

Inevitable. They were barbarians just like their mother.

Poor Holly!

I got into my coat, put a hat on my head and grabbed my purse, then ran outside to the Falcon.

Wouldn't you know it? The car wouldn't start.

It wasn't for lack of gas, either. Jonathan had taken both of our cars, one after the other, out early in the morning, the day before, as he did every Sunday, and filled up both tanks with gas.

The car probably wouldn't start because, once again, it was bitingly cold outside. I was no mechanic but figured that must have done something to mess with the car.

It took me several more attempts before I finally gave up on it. I could have wept. My child had gotten hurt because of me and now I couldn't even get right to her. I banged on the wheel but that didn't help.

I went back into the house to call Julie. She answered on the second ring and said she'd come right over to pick me up.

True to her word, she was there in only ten minutes, but they were ten agonizingly *long* minutes to me. Endless.

Gurgling little Joy was only a month old or so but was strapped into a car seat. I all but jumped into the front seat, I was that eager to get to the school, and sat beside the baby.

"Thanks for getting here so soon," I said breathlessly to my sister-in-law as I shut the car door, and off we went. We drove along Mayfair Drive and hung a left on Main Street to get to the school. "I can't bear the thought of Holly hurt with a broken arm, and in pain."

"Neither can I," Julie told me. "That poor child."

She and the baby came in with me when we got to the school since it was too cold out for them to wait in the car without the engine running. I worried that the baby was out and about, but what could we do? We reported to the main office to see the principal and get Holly out of there.

The two Nugent children were sitting on a bench in the secretary's room which was adjacent to of the principal's office. There was no sign of Lori, the secretary. Maybe, I couldn't help but think, she didn't want to be in the same room with Jack and Cecilia and had chosen that moment to go to the teacher's room for a coffee or had otherwise taken any opportunity to absent herself.

"Look who's here. It's the two yellow belly sap suckers' wacky violent mother," Jack Nugent snapped with a nasty little nod in my direction. "The adopter of the gooks."

"Jack Nugent!" Mrs. Reynolds came out of her office like a storm trooper on the march, looking furious at him and his words. "That's a terrible thing to say! Apologize to Mrs. O'Malley!" She was an older lady with snow white hair and gold wire-rimmed glasses. She looked like Mrs. Santa Claus without the red suit, but could be tough as nails on the kids if they had done anything to warrant it. Where these two were concerned, thank God somebody was.

"Why should he apologize? He didn't lie," Cecilia Nugent told Mrs. Reynolds in her usual smug tone. "Mrs. O'Malley is a nut! She went after our mother yesterday. She's bonkers, off the deep end. She kicked our mom, punched her and spit on her, too."

"That's a total lie," I said to the principal, "but I'll leave it to you handle the *severe* problem of the Nugent kids." After all, that sure wasn't my job. "Where's Holly?" Wherever she was, I was just glad it wasn't in the principal's office with Jack and Cecilia.

"I'll show you the way. You two stay here until your mother comes to pick you up," said Mrs. Reynolds briskly, leading us down the hallway to the room not much bigger than a closet that passed for the nurse's office. Holly was in there, lying on a cot with a tearstained face and wincing in pain. The school nurse had put an ice pack on her arm. From the look on Holly's face it wasn't helping very much.

"How ya doing, kid?" I asked her.

"I've had better days," Holly replied in a tone more appropriate for a world-weary grown woman than a little fifth grader.

"In a lot of pain?" Julie asked her.

She nodded.

"She's a trouper," said the school nurse kindly. "She's really hurt but she's trying to tough this out."

"Okay, we're going to get you to the doc's," I said to my daughter. "Ready to go?"

"I need my coat," Holly replied miserably.

"Of course you do. I'll go to your classroom and get it for you," I said. "Aunt Julie and your cousin Joy will stay here with you for a minute."

"Let me go with you," Mrs. Reynolds said, even though I knew my way to the room since I was the classroom mother. It was on the second floor. I tried not to let Mrs. Reynolds see how furious I was at the Nugent children for doing this to my daughter, and how mad I was at myself, besides, for having given them a reason to seek revenge on me through Holly in the first place.

"I believe in what you're trying to do, you know," Mrs. Reynolds said to me as we traversed the hallway to the staircase. "You and your husband are very kind people, taking Bonnie and Liana in the way you have and giving them a good home. More people should be doing the same, if you ask me, especially with regard to the Vietnamese orphans. But, Mrs. O'Malley, how shall I say this? There's something I think you ought to consider here."

"What's that?" I asked distractedly, thinking of the pain I'd just seen on my Holly's face.

"We had another family here at the school several years ago. The Lanscombes. They adopted a little boy from Korea and named him Teddy. He was a lovely child," she said as we reached the stairs and began to climb, "a darling little boy, but around here his appearance made him stick out like a sore thumb. Some of the children were very cruel to him for no other reason than that he looked Asian."

"They had no right to be," I decreed. "Can't the school do something to stop this sort of thing?"

"We try. I agree with you, we have to stop it when we see it whenever possible, and I intervened with the children who were giving him grief as much as I could, of course. In my position I didn't feel it was right to let the little bullies get away with their abuse. But when I brought it up to his parents, the Lanscombes, that he was being targeted because of his race, do you know what they said?"

We'd reached the top of the stairs. I shook my head no.

"They said, 'We're color-blind where race is concerned, and other people should be, too.'" She sounded outraged about it.

"That's not," I replied defensively, "a bad idea."

"Of course it isn't." The principal stopped walking as we got in front of Holly's classroom and faced me. I stopped in my tracks too.

"But you see, Mrs. O'Malley," she continued, "while the Lanscombes were, as they said, 'color-blind' about race, and while I'm sure you and your husband are as well, there are certain *other* people,

American people, that is, in this community, who aren't color-blind at all. Who just *aren't*. What they *ought to be* is one thing, but for those who haven't gotten there yet, that's really beside the point, isn't it? Right now, *this* is where and what those people *are*. Racists. People," she added softly, "like the Nugent family."

"That family is narrow-minded and prejudiced and extremely ignorant on top of all else," I fumed, "and they've raised their children to be just like them." If Sofia hadn't been all of those things I never would have tried to get even with her in the ice cream parlor in the first place, I thought, though I didn't add that.

"Yes, they are," she continued, "but I want you to understand something. They're not the only bigots in town. I would suggest that you do everything in your power to strengthen your children to be able to rise above this sort of thing, especially Bonnie and Liana, but Holly, too. Teddy Lanscombe was becoming completely demoralized by the stupid things other children said to him, and by always looking different."

"There isn't anything wrong with looking different," I said hotly. Couldn't she stop talking so we could just get that coat?

"No, there isn't. But it can take a real toll on the children who feel like they're not only different-looking but outnumbered."

"I'll keep all of this in mind," I told her impatiently, "but please, right now, I really only want to get Holly to the doctor, okay? Can we just get her coat and save this discussion for another day?"

"Of course! Here's the classroom."

We went inside. I found Holly's emerald green winter coat on a hook in the cloakroom. Her young teacher, Miss Kaminsky, fresh out of teacher's college, seemed distraught at what had happened and asked us how Holly was doing. I said we were about to get her to a doctor to find out for sure but that her arm seemed to be definitely broken.

And I want to get to my brother Alan the cop, right after we get to the doctor, I thought, and see if I can file an official police complaint against Cecilia and Jack Nugent. They were juvenile delinquents in training and shouldn't be allowed to get away with this.

As I went back downstairs with Mrs. Reynolds, holding the coat over my arm, I asked, "So what became of Teddy Lanscombe?"

She sighed. "He tried to kill himself when he got to junior high school, when I no longer had jurisdiction over the way he was treated, and the mockery over his race got worse."

"What!"

She nodded sadly. "Yes. He didn't succeed in doing himself in, of course, and after that the family moved away to Indianapolis, where they thought he wouldn't stand out quite so much, but that's what I'm trying to tell you. You've done the right thing by adopting those two Vietnamese girls. They're two of the luckiest kids in Emerson to have landed in as good a home as yours. But please. Be careful with them. Decent adoptive parents like you, the ones who are 'color-blind,' don't always realize how tough it can be on these kids of other races. Teddy took it all far too hard, and I really don't want to see anything similar happening to your children."

This was a lot for me to digest. I had not even thought twice about anything like that, and I suddenly wanted to ponder it further, but right at that particular moment, my main priority was first and foremost to get Holly to the doctor.

One problem at a time.

Chapter Sixteen

<u>Abducted!</u>

Holly could only get her good arm into the sleeve of her coat. I had to wrap the rest of it around her and bundled her out to the car, Julie with the baby in her arms beside us.

In my haste to get going I forgot to tell Mrs. Reynolds that I'd be back to pick up Bonnie and Liana when the school day was done, and that they shouldn't be walk home, or why I felt it was important that they didn't. That strange man with the scar was almost certainly still lurking around Emerson, after all. A quick look at my watch, when we got to the car, revealed it was only ten minutes after one o'clock. We had nearly two hours to get back and pick up the girls.

Holly settled into the backseat, lying across it. Julie almost broke the speed limit by getting us to Dr. Friedman's office.

Once there, his waiting room was packed with several kids who had the flu and their frazzled mothers. We were forced to wait for an hour before he was able to see Holly, despite the fact that her situation was an emergency. My poor child was in so much pain that she was unnaturally quiet in the waiting room. She didn't even want to look at the doctor's collection of *Highlights* magazines, though normally she loved to read that particular children's publication.

Nothing about today was even remotely normal.

It was also about to get far worse, though I didn't know that yet.

"Holly's arm definitely suffered a break," Dr. Friedman finally told us after examining her. "But I don't set broken arms. You need to get her to see Dr. Kent. He's a specialist in this sort of thing." Dr. Friedman wrote down an address for me. It was three towns away from Emerson.

Twenty minutes later we all arrived at Dr. Kent's office. He ushered Holly and me directly into an examination room, then brought us into an adjacent room for X-rays. The verdict? Her arm had been broken *in two places!*

Blast those rotten Nugents!

"Let me just make the plaster for a cast," Dr. Kent said, leading us back to the exam room, "and I'll be right back to fix this kid up, good as new." He winked at Holly. "You're being amazing about this, young lady. Just amazing." He seemed to be a very kind man.

Holly almost smiled at that.

"He's got that right," I said as he left the room.

"Oh! I forgot to tell you, Mom. That man from church, you know, Scarface? I think I saw him today."

Could matters become any crazier?

"You *what?*"

"I think I saw him. I was looking out my classroom window right before lunch. It's so cloudy out, I was hoping there might be some snow. A man just like him was standing right beyond the fence in front of the school, looking at the building. Wearing sunglasses."

"Aviator sunglasses?" I asked.

"Yes. I'm so sorry, Mom, I should've told you sooner, I just, you know, sort of forgot. With everything else going on."

"Being in pain can do that to you." I looked at the clock on the examining room wall, and oh my God! It was ten minutes to three, my other two children were soon to be dismissed from school – and I wasn't there! "Be right back, Holly. Sit tight."

I practically galloped into the waiting room, where Julie and Joy were patiently sitting on a bench by a picture window. "Julie! My God, I didn't realize, the other two will be waiting for me to pick them up in front of the school and I'm here, not there. Can I possibly impose on you further to get back there to pick them up?"

"Of course, Belinda. And then I'll bring them back here." She rose from her seat and put on her coat. "Don't worry."

"I can't not worry! Holly said that man was in front of the school today!" I didn't have to specify which one.

"Call Alan," she said as she went out the door, holding the baby. "Call the police station in Emerson and have him, or someone, go over there until I can get there!"

Dr. Kent's nurse let me use the phone.

Alan was not at his desk. He was off somewhere investigating a burglary.

I asked to speak to another officer. The one who came on the line was an Officer Bennett. I knew him. He was a good friend of Alan's, and had even been at barbecues my family had attended in the summertime at Alan and Julie's house. Officer Bennett said he'd get right over there to the school himself.

I thought that would be enough to take care of matters.

It would turn out I was wrong again.

"Mom, hey, where'd you go? Come back," Holly called out from the examination room.

I went back to her for a moment. "Just let me make another phone call, sweetie."

I went back to the reception area and this time called the school, trying to contact Mrs. Reynolds.

I wanted to tell her about the man Holly called Scarface and who had Liana terrorized for reasons she couldn't, or more like wouldn't, explain.

I planned to tell the principal to keep my daughters inside the building until Officer Bennett, and then their Aunt Julie, arrived.

But no one answered the phone! Not even when I let it ring ten times in a row.

I hung up, dialed again, and gave it another try.

Same result.

I thought back to earlier that afternoon when I had gone into the principal's office. It was like a two-room suite, with a secretary's desk in the portion right inside the door and the principal's office connected to it.

The secretary, a young gal called Lori, had not been behind her desk. It was Lori who usually answered the phone. Maybe, I'd thought, she had simply been in the bathroom or the teachers room.

Or on the other hand, now I was thinking perhaps she was out sick with that bad flu that was going around.

In any case, the phone wasn't answered. And I could easily figure out where Mrs. Reynolds probably was. The school was on the corner of Main Street and Alhambra Way. She would be outside of the building, not in front but on the Alhambra Way side, where most of the kids exited. She'd be there supervising the dismissal, as always.

She wouldn't be by the Main Street entrance. And that was where I'd given my children specific instructions to wait for me.

I tried to reach her on the phone one more time. It was no use.

My watch revealed it was now after three o'clock.

"Mom," Holly called out for me.

Officer Bennett was on the way to the school, at least. The police station was not too far away from there, so maybe he had even already arrived and it would all be all right.

And maybe, like an old neighbor originally from Europe used to say when I was a child and wishing didn't make something so, "If my grandmother had wheels, she'd be a pushcart."

"Mom!"

What could I do? I went to my daughter, just in time to watch Dr. Kent begin to put the cast on her arm.

⟫●⟪

Julie did not come back to Dr. Kent's office.

Holly and I waited.

And waited some more.

Holly's cast was on, the plaster dried, and Dr. Kent put her arm in a sling. Surely, I reasoned, Julie would be here any minute.

But she wasn't.

Holly and I sat down to wait for her in Dr. Kent's wedgwood blue waiting room, which for some reason was decorated with prints of horses. Only one other patient was there, and soon was called in to be seen.

Outside of the windows, it had started to snow rather heavily.

That's it, I thought. The snowstorm must be slowing Julie down.

That *had* to be it.

Nearly an hour went by and there was still no sign of Julie. None whatsoever.

She definitely should have been back with the girls by then. Where was she? I was starting to fly into an internal panic but tried to hide it from my daughter.

Holly was anxious to get home and I wanted to get her there. The kid needed to rest after such a bad day, and she needed some dinner, too, but what about my other two children? I realized something was definitely wrong.

The weather outside, now seen under the light of a streetlamp because darkness had fallen, had gotten worse. The storm had turned into a blizzard. I knew what that meant. Whiteout conditions were probably obscuring drivers' abilities to see through the snow on the roads.

Was Julie, along with the girls, stuck somewhere? That was the best case scenario. Or had she gotten into a car accident? That was the worst.

"Mrs. O'Malley," Dr. Kent finally came out front to the reception area to say, "we're going to be closing the office in another fifteen minutes. Can I have my assistant call you a cab?"

"I – I – I don't know. Can I make another phone call on your phone?"

"Of course. But I'm sorry. You're going to have to leave soon. I have a long drive home and it doesn't look like a promising night to be on the roads."

He didn't have to remind me.

Once again I dialed the number for Alan's police station. A cop I didn't know, Officer Tim Healy, answered the phone.

"You're Mrs. O'Malley? Belinda O'Malley, Alan's sister?"

"Yes," I replied, "may I speak to him?"

"You can't. He's out on an emergency call. We've been trying to reach you, Mrs. O'Malley."

"Why?" I asked.

"Your daughter Liana has been abducted."

"Abducted?" I nearly shrieked.

"Unfortunately, yes. From the school. Julie O'Malley is there with your daughter Bonnie, and your husband is enroute, too. Your brother is in charge of the investigation. Where are you, and how soon can you get over there to Emerson Elementary?"

Chapter Seventeen

<u>A Red-Haired Shrew in Purple and Blue</u>

I n the end we didn't have to take a cab at all. Officer Healy said he would come to Dr. Kent's office, get us and bring us back to Emerson himself.

I was like a proverbial train wreck. I was crying and shaking and as big a mess as I'd ever been in my life. Liana, kidnapped? *Stolen?* It was unfathomable, and yet, word was it had happened.

"What is it, Mom?" Holly asked, sounding like she was starting to panic, too. "What happened?"

I always liked to protect her from unpleasantries, but this time didn't want to *not* tell her the whole truth. "Liana's missing!"

"What?"

"She's missing. Abducted from the school. Taken! Oh, my God, Holly!"

"He's got her, then," she said, tears welling up in her eyes. "That man. The one who was at the church. He has her. It can't be anyone else."

"You're right," I agreed with her shakily. "It's got to be him. But why would a grown man be after my eight-year-old daughter?"

It was a question without an answer.

This was my fault.

All of it.

Every single bit.

I shouldn't have sent my children to school that day. Not after the situation with the man at the church and the way Liana had gotten so upset by his presence. Not after hearing from the Trinh grandmother that he had been showing my child's photograph from the newspaper to her, and asking around about Liana. I should have known from that point forward that my daughter was in extreme danger. Should have given all three kids an unofficial school holiday until we had this whole entire mess sorted out.

But no.

No, I'd sent them to school, as if they'd be safe there and it was just another normal day, as though nothing bad would ever befall any of them. If there was an award for the biggest idiot on the planet in January of 1976, I would have won it. What was I, born last week? Now I had one child missing, another one injured, and God only knew what was happening with the third. Bonnie. At least she was with her Aunt Julie and Uncle Alan, but even so. She'd had to watch the whole thing happen.

"Be sure to keep us posted," Dr. Kent's secretary told us. She'd heard everything and was appalled.

"Yes, please do," the doctor added. "And we'll keep the office open until your ride arrives. It's the least we can do."

Officer Tim Healy showed up faster than I had expected. He told us he'd used his police car's red lights and siren all the way to Dr. Kent's office. He kept the flashing lights on but spared us the noise of the siren all the way back to Emerson.

"According to Bonnie," he told us, "the two girls waited in front of the school for you, but you weren't there, and Julie was late getting to them. Officer Bennett was on the way but he hadn't arrived yet either when a woman came up to them. She was yelling in Vietnamese. Bonnie didn't have any idea who she was, she said she'd never seen her before, but Liana knew her. They got scared. Liana grabbed Bonnie by the hand and they tried to get inside the school doors, but the woman yanked them apart. She took Liana away, putting a knife to her head."

Liana. Little Liana, my sweet, pretty lotus blossom, was taken away from her school with *a knife* to her head? It was unfathomable. Unreal.

Yet a police officer was in the car with us, and he was telling us that it was true. "This can't," I said, "get worse."

"It just might," Officer Healy replied. He swerved on an icy road and had to fight with the wheel to right the car. My God, now we had the snow hazard to contend with on top of everything else. "You two need to be very strong."

"There was a strange man who seemed to have far too much of an interest in Liana," I told him.

"Yes, Alan and Julie filled us in about that."

"But not a woman. Who in the world could that be?"

"Ma'am, that's the question of the hour. Bonnie's been helpful, I hear. She understood what that psycho bitch said to Liana and gave Alan a translation."

"What did she say?" I asked.

"I don't know the particulars, just that she's been great."

I believed it. Bonnie wasn't reticent like Liana. Whatever she knew, she'd spill the beans and be happy to do so. Thank God for that! I felt we couldn't arrive at the school fast enough.

When we got there we found chaos. Several cop cars were parked out front and we found a lot of policemen inside of the building. Holly went to sit on the last of the seven steps leading up to the auditorium, looking spent, which she probably was. Mrs. Reynolds was still there in the building, very distraught. Her normally beautifully coiffed and sprayed hair was a flattened mess and she looked as though she'd been crying.

I found Bonnie sitting beside Julie on a bench in the outer section of the principal's office. It was a relief to see the child looked none the worse for wear. She was cradling baby Joy.

"Glad you're here," Julie said to me, "and I'm so sorry! The police stopped me from going back to Dr. Kent's for you. They asked me question after question about that odd man you mentioned, but whoever took Liana was a woman."

"So I just heard. What do you know?"

"It's this one," Julie said, nodding towards Bonnie, "who's the star witness."

"Hi, Mom," Bonnie said to me with a tiny smile. Then she gave the baby back to Julie, leapt off the bench, and hugged me tight.

I hugged her right back, as always, rocking her back and forth just the slightest little bit as we both stood there in the principal's office. I could only imagine what she had had to endure that afternoon, standing outside in the freezing cold, as Liana was led away by what sounded like a maniac in the truest sense of the word. Who but a complete lunatic would have pulled a knife on an eight-year-old girl? If I ever got my hands on the dragon who did this, I'd be hitting her with a lot more than a simple hot fudge sundae.

"Let's go for a little walk down the hallway," I suggested to Bonnie. I kept one arm around her as we strolled in the direction of her classroom. The kids had made Valentine's Day decorations which were already hanging up on a bulletin board outside of the room with lots of red and pink hearts made from construction paper and trimmed with paper lace doilies. The children had written what they loved the most on the hearts. On Bonnie's she had carefully printed "I love my family" in purple magic marker.

She pointed to it.

"We love you right back," I told her, giving her a sideways squeeze. She smiled at that. "I know, Mom."

"And I need you to tell me everything that happened today. When you were outside waiting for me. Okay? Everything you remember."

"Lady came. She looked okay. She was American, and had orange hair. Blue and purple coat, squares and lines. She say, I mean *said*, in Vietnamese, 'Happy I see you Lien.' Not Liana. *Lien*. Didn't sound like she was happy. Sounded mad. Lady said, 'You know why I'm here. What you have to do.' Liana looked scared, tried to go inside, and pull me in too. The lady moved fast. She took out a big knife. Said, 'No, you come with me.'" Bonnie pantomimed holding a knife to my neck. "Like that. Took Liana away. Liana was crying."

Oh, I could just bet she was.

This was monumentally disturbing.

To make matters even worse, the monstrous excuse for a human being had said the child knew why she was there.

And was supposed to know *what she had to do.*

It was like what Bonnie had told me in the ice cream parlor the day before. Was it only yesterday? It seemed like forever ago. But Bonnie had said that Liana had a "secret mission."

As outrageous a claim as that was, it was actually panning out.

Whatever could it be?

"Did Liana say anything when the shrew, I mean *the lady*, showed up?" I asked. "Like did she say the woman's name, by any chance?"

"No."

"Then what happened? Did they walk away?"

"No. A car took them. Blue car."

"A blue car?"

"Yes. I think man from church was driving."

"The one with the scar on his face and the sunglasses, honeybunch? That man?"

"Yes. That one."

Now we were getting somewhere. So the two of them were in this together, Scarface and the shrew. But what was this?

We turned around to walk back toward the principal's office. "What were you saying about the lady having orange hair? Was she an American?"

Bonnie nodded. "Maybe. I think so. Bright orange hair."

"Are you telling me this vixen was a white American lady?"

"Yes. But she spoke Vietnamese."

Oh, it got stranger by the minute! An American redhead speaking Vietnamese was the abductor? How many could there be who fit that description and were wandering around in Emerson, Indiana?

"What were you saying about the coat this lady wore?" I asked. "You said it was blue and purple and with lines and squares?"

Bonnie nodded. "Yes."

"Do you mean on the pattern of the coat? What was on the material?"

The child looked confused. "I don't know. Pattern?"

Of course she didn't know that word yet. Why would she? It wasn't something a child of seven going on eight, from another land, probably ever had to consider before in her life.

"Could you try and draw it for me?" I asked her. I had a feeling I knew what she was referring to but had to make absolutely certain.

"Yes, sure!"

Once in the office, I found a piece of paper on the secretary's desk and a pen for Bonnie to use. She proceeded to draw what looked like an approximation of a pattern of plaid.

Just as I thought.

"Ah, plaid! That's what you're saying! That's called plaid, honeybunch. Did you tell the police about the coat?"

"Yes. But I just tell them blue and purple."

"That's okay. You probably didn't mention it was blue and purple plaid if you're unfamiliar with the term. Let me show this to Uncle Alan."

I took the sketch and all but ran over to where my brother was conferring with the chief of police and three other cops. They were in a classroom across the hall.

"The woman involved in this," I reported, interrupting the chief, who was in the middle of a sentence, "was wearing a plaid coat. Bonnie just drew this illustration."

"Oh, is that what she meant before about the coat? This is good," Alan told me. "This will help us narrow it down even further."

"Did Bonnie also tell you the woman had bright red hair and is possibly an American, but spoke Vietnamese and called Liana 'Lien?'"

Alan nodded. "She sure did. We've got an all-points bulletin out for Liana right now, that ghastly red-haired gal who pulled the knife on her, and for the Vietnamese man with the scar, too. I have a feeling those three will look like a memorable trio, for sure. It's not going to be easy for them to get anyplace with Liana tonight. Not in this blizzard. We've got cops checking every hotel and motel in the area. We have the news media involved, television and radio. We've even gotten the word out that Liana was kidnapped by an Asian man and an American woman and, as Bonnie told us, rode away in a blue car. If only she knew what make and model! But she doesn't."

"We can't have everything," the chief chuckled. "Bonnie's only a little girl, not a car expert, but she's already been a champion as a witness."

I went over to the steps to the auditorium to see how Holly was doing. Her teacher, Miss Kaminsky, had not gone home. She was sitting there with Holly, keeping her company. She'd brought her some books, Bobbsey Twins mysteries. Holly loved those.

"Holly seems exhausted," Miss Kaminsky said to me, "and I live right across the street on Alhambra Way. Why don't I take her home for the night and give her some dinner? She can sleep over and I'll get her to school in the morning."

"That would be lovely of you," I said. "Yes, by all means." They soon left.

So did Julie and the baby. "I have to get Joy home. She's been too long without any formula and now she's getting cranky."

"Of course," I said. "You've been amazing today, Julie."

She shrugged off the compliment. "We're family. Just be sure to call me the minute Liana is found."

Jonathan arrived, all but bursting, along with an amazingly strong gust of wind, in through the school's main doors. "What the hell is going on?" He roared. "I've been hearing all kinds of be on the lookout radio bulletins regarding my daughter Liana all the way back here from Indianapolis!"

It took some time to fill him in on the whole horrifying story. How Holly had been hurt, I was about to pick her up, and then my car wouldn't start. Julie's help. One doctor sending us to the other. Ending up with its being too late when Julie went to pick up the other two girls. And then, Liana's abduction, and Bonnie's eyewitness report.

"This was the worst day of my whole life," I finally wrapped it all up for Jon. I sobbed for a few minutes and he held me in his arms.

"Okay," he said, "let's go talk with the police."

"So far they haven't gotten much of anywhere with it yet, so don't get your hopes up."

It was then that I remembered how, initially, I had spent a large portion of that morning waiting for Marianne from the adoption agency to call me back. She was going to speak with the director of Liana's orphanage, Sister Elizabeth, to see if there was any more information she could give to us about the child we'd adopted and loved so dearly, but couldn't entirely understand. I'd had to leave the house when I heard what had happened to Holly before Marianne had had a chance to call me back.

"Jonathan," I said, "I just realized. I think there might just be somebody in California who may be able to shed some light on this mess we're in."

"Well for God's sake," Jonathan replied, "pray tell me who it is."

Chapter Eighteen

A Message from Mrs. Delmonico

We strode straight into the classroom where Alan was still conferring with the chief of police and, now, six or seven other concerned officers. They were discussing trying to mount a search party to look for my daughter, snow or no snow.

"It's probably not going to be too effective in this kind of weather," the chief was saying. "Especially since they drove away with the girl in a car and didn't take her while they were on foot. They could be anywhere by now. Anywhere. Even at the airport or the train station. It's been a few hours already so they could even be well away from Indiana."

"Or they could be right here," one of the cops replied, "at the motel over on Flora Street."

"It was already checked," said the chief, "and so far they haven't shown up there."

"Damn!" Alan swore. "But then, that would be too easy, wouldn't it? If we were to find them nearby."

"Alan," I said, "I have a suggestion. The director of Liana's orphanage lives in a convent in Los Angeles now. I think we need to call her and find out what she might be able to tell us about Liana. Bonnie said yesterday that Liana knew the man who's involved in this in Saigon."

"Now that," Alan said, "is a good idea." We went back to the principal's office, first to call Marianne, and then to get the number from her for Sister Elizabeth. I was no longer going to wait for Marianne to get the information for us. I said to Alan that I wanted to speak to the nun directly.

"Sorry, Sis, but I'm the one who is going to be talking to her directly," Alan insisted. "As part of this investigation. You can talk to Marianne first and get the woman's number, but I have to take it from there."

I dialed Marianne. She answered after a few rings. "Oh, hi, Belinda. I tried to contact you a few times this afternoon but couldn't reach you."

"Marianne, it's a long story, but we've got a major problem here." Marianne lived in Chicago, not Indiana, so she probably hadn't heard the local news reports. "Liana's been abducted. The man with the scar and an American woman have her. Apparently Liana knew the man in Saigon but that's all we know. I'm here with the police, and we need Sister Elizabeth's number right now."

"That's hideous!"

"Tell me about it."

"All right, sure. Hold on a sec and let me get the number." She was back on the phone within a minute, rattling off a number that I wrote down on a pad on Lori's desk. "Please call me back when you find the child."

The number had a 213 area code. Alan dialed. We waited for the phone to be answered.

It wasn't.

He hung up, and tried the number again.

The same thing happened. No one answered.

"That's odd," I observed. "She lives in a convent. You would think somebody would answer the phone there."

He gave it one more attempt before giving up for the moment.

"Let me have Tim Healy see what he can find out about this convent," Alan finally said. "This is urgent, so I'll ask him to reach out to the archdiocese of Los Angeles."

Alan left the room in search of Tim Healy. Jonathan went with him. Bonnie had fallen asleep on the bench and stayed there in the secretary's part of the office. I folded up her coat and arranged it under her sleepy head like a pillow. I should have asked Julie to take her home with her.

I went to sit on the few steps leading up to the auditorium, just wanting a moment to myself and some time to think.

God, what a day! Nothing seemed to be going easily, to say the least of it, let alone working out. I felt emotionally exhausted yet all wired up at the same time. I couldn't even think of resting until we got Liana back.

It was entirely possible, I knew, that we'd never see that precious child again. We didn't know what those people who had her wanted, or if they planned to give her back.

Bonnie's account of the words of the shrew in the blue and purple plaid coat came back to me. The creature had said to Liana, "You know why I'm here. What you have to do."

That seemed to indicate that Liana knew her already, as well as the man, didn't it? Where might she have known a red-haired American woman from? A lot of Americans had lived in Vietnam, from what I heard, not only members of the military. Who had this one been to Liana?

No, not to Liana. To Lien. That's what Bonnie said she called her. The plaid-clad dragon lady must have known the child somewhere back in Vietnam, then, if she didn't know her new American name.

It didn't help to know that my information about Liana's past only extended to her mother leaving, Liana being thrown out of their apartment and living out in the elements, and then her arrival at the orphanage.

I had so many questions. Where had her mother's apartment been? What was the name of their Saigon neighborhood, for starters? Not that I knew one section of Saigon from another. I didn't. I'd never been there. But if I knew even that much, like what kind of a home Liana had had, and where it had been, it might have given me at least a hint of what type of lifestyle she and her mother may have enjoyed. We basically had *no* information about Liana. Was her mother wealthy? Poor? Employed? Struggling? What?

It didn't, or at least it wouldn't have, mattered one way or the other under normal circumstances. She was my child now, period.

But in light of the fact that those two weirdos had taken her away today, absolutely any information might just have been a help in figuring out what was behind this crime.

And who, not to mention where, was her father?

That made me wonder some more about the man with the scar. Was it at all possible that *he* might be Liana's father?

Well, anything was possible, really, but if he was, why was he hanging out in front of the Presidio, and on Fisherman's Wharf, and at our church, watching her? Why didn't he just go inside the Presidio, right from the start, and say, "I'm the father of that little girl and I'm here to claim her?"

He hadn't.

That was enough to lead me to believe she wasn't his daughter.

Besides, Liana herself said she didn't know who that man was when we had asked her. Surely the child would have recognized her own dad.

On the other hand, he'd told Grandma Trihn that he was her *uncle*.

Again, though. If he was really and truly related to Liana he should have spoken up, claimed her, and had done with it. The fact that he didn't, and preferred to sneak around, watching her or asking people questions about her, said volumes. I was willing to bet he was neither relative nor friend and had no rights to Liana whatsoever. He should not be anywhere near her at all.

But he had her in his clutches at the moment.

And he and the red-headed shrew wanted her to do something for them.

I got up off the steps and started to pace back and forth. This was all so frustrating. Mrs. Reynolds, still on the premises, offered to make me a cup of coffee in the teachers' room, and I said that would be great, not even caring if the caffeine wired me up any further.

Officer Tim Healy found me. "I reached the archdiocese in Los Angeles," he said, concern all over his freckled face. "That number the agency lady gave you? It's not to a convent. Not any convent they've ever heard of, anyway."

"It's not?" That was surprising. "I'm sure I wrote down the number just the way Marianne Bigsby dictated it to me."

"Let me have this Marianne's number, would you? I'll call her back and make sure you got it right."

I rattled it off and he went back into the office to dial Marianne.

At that point, as I strode back and forth along the hallway with jangling nerves, waiting for Mrs. Reynolds to come back with the coffee, there was some action with the cops.

First the chief of police came by and said, "I think we need to move base camp and go back to the police station. There's not much else we can do here."

He was about to leave and take several policemen with him when Alan received a communication via walkie-talkie.

My neighbor, Mrs. Delmonico, had seen that Liana was missing on the TV news. She'd also seen something else and she called police headquarters about it. The dispatcher notified Alan.

My brother came charging over to me. "Angie Delmonico just reported there's a car in your driveway," he reported. "She heard glass breaking, and there are lights on in your house. Somebody's in there. Maybe thieves, or maybe the people who have Liana."

"What?" It was all I could manage to say when I heard *that*. Our house was being robbed, and Angie Delmonico, of all people, had been the one to call it in to help us? In a day full of unpleasant surprises, I could not believe what I was hearing *now*.

"Someone's broken into your house. If we're lucky, it's the people who have your daughter. You stay here." He called out to the other cops, "Chief, Tim, Charlie, Roger, let's go! The rest, stay here!"

The cops grabbed their coats and gear and rushed out of the building into the storm.

Mrs. Reynolds came along with my coffee.

I took a quick sip, filled her in on the latest, and went to find Jonathan. "Have you heard what they're saying?"

"Yes. We need to sit tight."

"I want to get home to the house, Jon. I don't want to stay here, for heaven's sake, while God knows what is going on over there."

"Absolutely not. Let the cops take care of it."

"Do you think it's the people who took Liana?"

"At this point? I don't know what to think."

I didn't either.

But suddenly I felt a tiny spark of hope.

Chapter Nineteen

<u>A Certain Doll</u>

Two cops stayed back at the school while we waited. One of them had taken over the main office and was trying to find out more information about Liana's orphanage. He didn't seem to be making progress. Bonnie was still in there on the bench, sleeping through it. As for the other cop, I wasn't sure what he was supposed to be doing. He just seemed to be hanging around in one of the classrooms, keeping his walkie-talkie on. Every now and then it seemed to squawk loud enough to wake the dead. Each time it made any noises my nerves were shot all over again.

Mrs. Reynolds got some coffee for Jonathan, too, and had a can of Coca-Cola ready for Bonnie, if she were to awake. I was glad the kid was out cold and missing a lot of this madness.

After that, Mrs. Reynolds, Jon and I sat down on the miniature kiddie chairs in one of the classrooms, not in the same one where the officer with the noisy walkie-talkie had ensconced himself, and waited.

And waited.

And waited some more.

God, what a dreadful day.

Mrs. Reynolds told me some more about little Teddy Lanscombe, the Korean child who had been adopted and had gone to the school years earlier. She was in touch with the family. Perhaps, she suggested, we could get together with them sometime. I said I would like that.

But that was if all went well.

If Liana came home.

If she didn't end up lost to us forever. *Don't let that happen, God. Bring her home.*

"What in the world could be going on at our house?" I said at one point. "If it isn't the horrid people who took Liana who broke in, then who is it?"

"Could be thieves," Jonathan said, "just regular old-fashioned garden-variety crooks, who heard our daughter was missing on the news and figured we wouldn't be home. Taking advantage of what they hoped was an opportunity."

"Despicable, if that's what it is," observed Mrs. Reynolds.

"You must be tired and want to go home," I said to her. "I'm so sorry this is keeping you here."

"Nonsense," she replied. "Do you think I would go anywhere else with a crisis like this going on? I want to find out where Liana is just like you do. She's one of our Emerson Elementary School children. They're all precious to me, you know."

"I can believe it. But even the Nugent kids?"

She shrugged. "Let's just say some are more precious than others."

It was an hour and fifteen never-ending long drawn out minutes before the cop in the other classroom got the notification on the walkie-talkie that we'd been waiting for, hoping for, and praying for, too.

He came into the room looking jubilant. "They found her," he exulted. "They found your daughter Liana!"

"What?" Mrs. Reynolds said in surprise.

"Hallelujah," I breathed.

"Well, it's about time," Jonathan said, and started to laugh.

All three of us started high-fiving one another. I was laughing and crying all at the same time.

Bonnie woke up, came out of the principal's office, and joined us, high-fiving and laughing and hugging us, one after the other, even Mrs. Reynolds, too.

We were all jubilant, including the cop who'd gotten the news. He was a very young man and had tears in his eyes.

"I was so afraid she was a goner," he admitted. "Meanwhile, Alan told me to get all of you into my squad car, and that I should take you to the police station. He'll meet you there with Liana, and they'll be bringing the perpetrators in, too. He especially told me to give you a heads up about that."

Jonathan said, "Yes, because he knows I'd like five minutes with each one of those creeps. I'd love to put a baseball bat up each one of their asses."

Bonnie seemed to fully understand that. She laughed out loud, and it came to us as a sparkling sound, the sunlight shining through the clouds after the storm.

"Me too. At the very least," I agreed about the baseball bat, though of course, we'd never really do anything like that. Which didn't mean they didn't deserve it.

"And me," said Bonnie.

"Oh, we're just kidding, darling," I said, giving her a hug. The last thing I wanted her to think we could ever be serious about involved baseball bats and orifices. After all, we weren't like the Nugents.

"Let me just lock up the school for the night," Mrs. Reynolds said, "and if you'd have me, I'd like to go with you."

"Of course," Jonathan said. "You've been terrific to us with all this insanity going on."

Outside in the fresh but freezing cold air we found that the snowstorm had abated somewhat, but it was still going on. There already seemed to be six fresh new inches of snow on the ground since it had started that afternoon, nice, pure snow.

The night was peaceful. *Finally.*

"We have to call the teacher's house when we get to the station," I said to Mrs. Reynolds, "so Holly knows what's going on."

"It will be my pleasure to make that call to Miss Kaminsky," she smiled.

"And I'll call Julie and Marianne, too," I said.

We piled into the car, with Jon sitting in front with the cop, whose name was Arnie Foster, and Mrs. Reynolds and me in the back, Bonnie sitting in the middle, between us.

"I'm going to drive slowly," Arnie said, "in case the streets are icy."

"So long as we get there," I said. "I can't wait to see Liana!"

———◉———

Liana was already sitting behind Alan's desk in his office, eating Hostess Twinkies, when we arrived.

She jumped right up and ran to Jonathan, Bonnie, and me with her arms open wide. "Mommy! Daddy! Bonnie!" She'd never been so effusive before.

All of us hugged her, all three together.

"Are we ever glad to see you," I told her when we'd all let go. I immediately reached for her again to keep on hugging her tight, so relieved to see her, alive, well, and there with those Twinkies, that I started to cry. I couldn't help it. Neither could Jonathan. There had been a very real possibility that this child might very well have been killed tonight by those awful people.

There were tears in Liana's eyes too. "I was scared. She had a knife."

"We heard," I said, "but everything is all right now." At least I hoped it was. This poor kid would probably be affected by the events of this day for the rest of her life. I'd do what I could to try and lessen the impact of them on her as much as possible.

Mrs. Reynolds came into the office to join us then. "I've just called Miss Kaminsky. She and Holly are overjoyed. They'd come over if it wasn't for the snow. Hello there, Miss Liana!"

Liana let go of me and ran over to the principal and gave her a big hug, too. Then she hugged her little sister again, and then Jonathan.

All of us sat down on the chairs in Alan's office. I pulled Liana onto my lap and it was one of those moments when I felt it would be great to never to let her go again.

We had another endlessly long wait in there while Alan and his team of detectives interrogated the two creeps who'd taken Liana. Officer Healy came into the room with burgers and fries that he'd gone out and gotten for us at a little restaurant next door to the station. We were ravenous by then and welcomed the food.

It was well over an hour and a half later when Alan finally came into the room, smiling. "They're booked! They've also confessed. I've got them parked in our holding cell and they will be transferred to the county jail as soon as someone from county can get out here to Emerson to cart them away, hopefully for the rest of their lives, since kidnapping is a federal offense. With the storm still going on and the streets in a mess, county might not get here until the morning. Ha, let the two of 'em wait."

"Just who," I had to ask, "are they, anyway, this man and woman from hell who had the nerve to abduct our daughter?"

That's when I noticed what my brother had in his hand and put down on his desk.

It was the Vietnamese doll Liana had brought with her on the airplane during Operation Babylift. The one with the porcelain face and the cloth body that was dressed in the red and white *ao dai* and wore a conical hat.

What was *that* doing here?

"The guy," Alan explained, "is called Cuong Tran. Or maybe it's Tran Cuong, since in their culture, it's last names first, not first names first. That's a bit of a muddle at the moment. In any event, his vicious bitch of an accomplice already told us quite a bit of information about him and what they had going on. He was a petty thief in Nam who also managed to sometimes get a job as a van driver for the orphanage Liana was in, Star of the Sea. Cuong is the one who found Liana sleeping in the street, in front of a Saigon noodle shop, and brought her to that orphanage in the first place. Cuong himself managed to get here on the Babylift by saying he was a member of the orphanage staff."

"An orphanage staff member who was a petty thief?" Jonathan shook his head at the outrageousness of it. "They should have left him there to the communists."

"He's not a relative of Liana's," I asked, "is he?" That was my first question. I had been afraid, all along, that he was, and that maybe she'd been taken for that reason.

"Oh, no. He's no relation. Just a jerk who went on a few wild capers with her biological mother," Alan said.

"That's a relief," I sighed. "He told Grandma Trinh he was her uncle, and the very idea made my blood run cold."

"There's more, though," Alan told us, practically with a groan. "Whoa, folks, I've gotta tell you, there's a *whole lot* more."

"I can believe it," I said.

"Like I was saying, Cuong who recognized Liana when she was on the street. He had known her mother. He knew that her mother was dead. She, ah, was, shall we say, not exactly the most moral of people, if you read me." My brother didn't want to spell it out in front of Liana and Bonnie, but I could just imagine. "In fact, she was in the same unofficial profession as Cuong was."

Another thief, in other words.

"When he recognized Liana, he did not tell her that her mother was gone for good, but led her to believe she was still alive and well, and waiting for her in America. He also gave her this thing." He gestured distastefully toward Liana's doll on his desk. "She wasn't told the secret of this doll. She was just given an order to protect it.

"From what?" I asked.

Alan didn't answer that right away. Instead, he continued, "Cuong's accomplice, the red devil, told Liana not to tell anyone there was a reason she had the doll. She was just to shut up about it and protect it, take it with her when Star of the Sea was evacuated, and if she did all that, eventually, he said, she'd be reunited with her mother. If she lost the doll, though, she told her she'd never see her mother again. What an empty threat *that* was. All the while, the mother was already dead."

"Good God! I can hardly believe such a vicious level of cruelty!" I let that escape from my astonished mouth. *"Why?"*

"Show them, Liana."

Still on my lap, Liana reached for the doll on the desk and pulled it toward her. She lifted up the red dress of the *ao dai*.

The doll's cloth stomach had been cut open and then stitched back up with light blue thread. It was a ten-inch long cut. A few of the stitches at the top had already been pried open and I could see that it looked as though some milky rocks were in there.

"Diamonds. The evidence squad will be opening this thing later and photographing the contents. Cuong," Alan continued, "made a killing right before the moment he found Liana on the street. Saigon was in an uproar by then. The North Vietnamese Army was coming in and people were getting out of there any way they could, and that included a couple who owned a gem store, who had basically abandoned ship. Cuong got in there and helped himself to whatever they'd left behind. Apparently this doll was cut open and is stuffed with a whole collection of uncut gems."

For once in my life I was absolutely speechless.

"This Cuong character basically turned my daughter into an unwitting *smuggler?"* Jonathan asked in shock.

"In a word," said Alan, "yes."

I thought back to the moment we'd first met Liana in San Francisco.

How she'd argued with the translator about going with us, saying she had a reason to stay at the Presidio, which none of us understood.

How she'd seemed rather reluctant to be adopted at first, even as she also seemed glad to meet us. Torn.

The way she'd had night terrors, and also had been so unwilling to answer our specific questions about her past, and about the man we now knew was Cuong Tran, or maybe, Tran Cuong.

Then there had been her attempt at running away from home, when she had put two bucks, her doll and her Spirograph set into a tote bag and planned to flee the house. I'd thought she was running *away* from Cuong with her two favorite treasures and two dollars cash, but no, that probably wasn't it. When she said she had to go away, after hearing all of this, it seemed more likely she was thinking of running *toward* someone - her mother. That she had to get to Cuong, give him the doll, and in exchange, she and her mom would finally be able to be reunited.

She only abandoned that idea when we said she was ours and we would never let her go. Perhaps she had already sensed, by then, that if her mother, who was supposedly here in America, hadn't managed to find her already, then she wasn't coming.

It made sense now. Liana had initially thought if she kept that doll safe it would lead her to her missing mother.

Which was probably why she made sure to get the doll before she left the Presidio and bring it along with her. It was maybe even why the child often talked to the doll, too, first in her native language and then in her new one.

This good, sweet child had been left all alone with her thoughts, living through a horror story, right under our noses and in our own house, during all of this time. Nothing she did was going to bring her mother back to life no matter what the poor kid had done with that doll. I had to control my voice because the whole creepy scenario was enough to make me scream, and if I was on the verge of shouting about it, I could only imagine what my child was feeling. I had to take some deep breaths before I spoke.

"Seems a bit extreme, though," I finally calmed down enough to say. "Okay, they used Liana to get the doll out of Vietnam, but then, why did they ask *her*, specifically, to carry it in the first place? She might have been adopted into a family just about anywhere in the free world. Once she got here, they would have to track her down in order to retrieve it."

"That, as I'll explain," Alan said, "wasn't supposed to be as complicated as it became. They simply thought that it would look better, less suspicious, for a child, a little girl, to get on the plane with the doll, than it would be to have an adult carry it, especially when you consider the contents. That damn thing is filled with stolen property that's probably worth thousands and thousands of dollars."

"What about the woman who threatened my child with a knife?" Jonathan asked. "What's *her* story?"

"Oh, that's the best part," Jonathan told us. "Wait until you hear this! You aren't going to believe it. Fasten your seatbelts! Cuong's accomplice? That's none other than Sister Elizabeth, the former director of the Star of the Sea Orphanage."

"What!" Mrs. Reynolds and I chorused.

"Are you kidding me?" Jonathan asked in disbelief.

"She's in this with him up to her neck. She also flew to this country, to San Francisco, on Operation Babylift, and thought it would be easy to just grab the doll back from Liana once they landed and have done with it. But as it turned out, that wasn't possible. Sister Elizabeth arrived in bad health, with severe stomach pains, maybe partially brought on by the stress of having to evacuate a whole orphanage. She went straight to the emergency room at San Francisco General Hospital where she was diagnosed with appendicitis and had to have surgery. She didn't get her grubby hands on the doll, or know where Liana had been sent, once she got released from the hospital, which was a major problem for the duo. If not for her burst appendix, she would have nabbed the doll back and, failing that, was also supposed to be on the inside track of who adopted Liana. Again though, the initial plan was to just take the doll back ride off into the sunset with Cuong."

"This is unreal," I breathed, but knew it wasn't. "Sister Elizabeth told Marianne she had no idea who brought Liana to Star of the Sea."

Alan shrugged. "She lied." He continued, "By the time she got sprung from the hospital, Liana was already living with you, and Sister Elizabeth had not had access to where she'd been placed. She could not find out, at first, where the child went. Cuong kept an eye on things, meanwhile. He was only a sometimes van driver at the orphanage, not an official or a social worker, so while he got on the plane as if he was part of the staff, once here he was free to go. He hung around the Presidio. He would have snatched the doll away from Liana if she had come out of there carrying it herself, but it was Jonathan who had the children's belongings in hand. He couldn't tackle Jonathan and mug the kids' stuff away from him without looking mighty suspicious. Cuong tried to follow you on foot from the Presidio, to see what hotel you went to, but you left in a cab and he couldn't. He overheard Jonathan saying the next day you'd go to Fisherman's Wharf."

"That's right," Jonathan nodded. "That's exactly what I was saying when we left the Presidio, and I was carrying the girls' stuff in two plastic bags."

"The next day Cuong saw you at Fisherman's Wharf, too, but again, you left in a cab and he was on foot. He had to give up, at least temporarily. Elizabeth, meanwhile, soon relocated to Los Angeles, and then she and Cuong had to find Liana to try and get the doll back. But then at Christmastime that article about your family went out on the Associated Press wire and they finally had a target location for this wonderful kid here." He smiled in Liana's direction.

"They better put that shrew away," I said, "and for a good long time. How did you figure out she was Sister Elizabeth in the first place?"

"Officer Healy got suspicious," my brother said, "when he called the Los Angeles diocese and they said that the number you'd been given, Belinda, for the nun's convent was inaccurate. She wasn't at a convent out in L.A. Any convent. She was no longer even a nun. She'd already broken ties with the church ages ago, but managed to keep her post in Vietnam until the end, somehow. Underneath her nun's veil, her hair was flaming red. That phone number you were given, Belinda, was for her apartment on Hollywood Boulevard. By the time we were trying to reach her on the phone, Sister Elizabeth, real name Elsa Roth, had already flown here, to see about helping Cuong get the doll out of Liana. Incredibly, Cuong the thief and Elsa the ex-nun are boyfriend and girlfriend."

"What a combination," Jonathan said under his breath. "Some nun she is! The church must be relieved as all get-out to be rid of her."

"So the duo came to town and tracked Liana to the school. When they finally grabbed her, they figured it would be easy to get the doll back from her." Then he smiled at my daughter. "But Liana here wouldn't tell them where it was."

I hugged her once again. "That's my girl!"

Liana finally piped up. "They wanted my doll. Asked where it was. I said no. Not 'til I see my mother. Other mother," she explained apologetically, turning to face me while still on my lap.

"I understand, honeybunch," I told her, giving her a squeeze. What a thing to let her believe would happen!

"Then Sister Elizabeth said, 'Ha ha, too late, your ma is dead, been already dead a long time. Give me your doll.' But I wouldn't. Not when I heard *that*."

"I wouldn't have either," agreed Mrs. Reynolds.

"Neither would I," Jonathan chimed in.

"And you know I wouldn't have," I added. Or if I had, I would have hit the ex-nun over her head with it.

"This kid," Alan smiled, "is a marvel of inner strength, if you ask me."

"A superhero," Jonathan smiled at her. "Kid, we ought to call you Wonder Woman."

"How did they find the way to our house in the first place?" I asked.

"Elsa, or Sister Elizabeth, found your address in the phone book, that's how, so they reasoned the doll had to be somewhere in your house," Alan said. "By the time we got there, Elsa was threatening Liana with the knife in the living room while Cuong had gone upstairs to find the damn doll. We interrupted their search party."

"Incredible," I breathed.

And while it may have only been January, I figured *that* already qualified as the biggest understatement of 1976.

Chapter Twenty

<u>A Whole Lot of Hoopla</u>
February 1976

There was a whole lot of hoopla after that.

Television and newspaper reporters covered the story. We received lots of requests for interviews and even agreed to a few of them. All three of the kids were hailed as heroes, Holly for alerting me that Cuong had been hovering around the front of the school on the day he took Liana captive, Bonnie for her eyewitness testimony, and Liana, most of all, for resisting her captors and not wanting to hand over the doll. They enjoyed being on television, feeling like junior celebrities.

For a few days our story was big news in Indiana, and then it died back down again, replaced by stories like the ones about this Southern upstart who was gaining popularity with voters, Jimmy Carter.

I baked a large chocolate cake for Angie Delmonico and her whole family in order to thank her for having the good sense to call the police when she saw our house had been broken into. I didn't want to think about what might have happened to Liana if Angie hadn't called them at the exact moment when she did.

But she had.

I celebrated Liana's return by going on a shopping spree for the kids, getting them some new clothes, new hair barrettes and hair ties, and even new shoes. I had the idea that it would symbolically assist them in making a fresh start after all the turmoil that had happened, and while outfitting them in new duds wasn't exactly any kind of a cure-all, I figured it could at least help. All three of them had been traumatized, after all, Holly with the attack by the Nugent brats, Bonnie with witnessing the abduction of Liana, and Liana most of all.

I was very concerned about Liana in particular. It wasn't just from the whole craziness with regard to the doll full of stolen jewels or the fact that she'd been threatened the way she had. It was also the whole sick number that had been done on her head by Cuong and Elizabeth, telling her that her mother was alive, and that there was a way back to her if she did what they said, when she wasn't. It had been pure evil for those two psychopaths to do such a thing to such a wonderful little girl.

On the other hand, ever since she'd been rescued from Cuong and Sister Elizbaeth/Elsa Roth, she had become a lot more calm, and even warmed up to us considerably, too. Like she was finally allowing herself to fully settle in with us. There wasn't another mother out there, somewhere, waiting for her to come home. Now *this* was home. She even told us about her life before coming here, not in an orphanage, but living in a small apartment near the restaurant and bar where her mother was a hostess. That had been her mother's official job.

We didn't ask her about any of her mother's other activities, but from what Cuong told the authorities, Liana's mother had been, incredibly, a rather accomplished pickpocket and a cat burglar.

If Cuong could be believed, that is.

One night in early February, as Liana and I were cutting out pink paper hearts to make some Valentine's Day decorations, I casually brought up the subject of the vicious lies she had been fed by Cuong and Sister Elizabeth, all designed to get her to cooperate with carrying the doll full of gems. "You understand, don't you," I asked her in as gentle a town as I could muster, while also trying not to cry as I said it, "that Cuong and Elizabeth deliberately lied to you about your other mother, the other mother you had in Vietnam? That it was all a ruse?" Then, not sure if she was familiar with that particular vile little term, I clarified, "A tall tale told to keep you under control and get you to comply with the situation about the doll?"

"Yes," she answered quietly, and in ever-improving English. "I'm so sorry I believed them."

"You don't have to be sorry, honeybunch. You didn't know what they said wasn't true when they said it. Okay? But you know something? Your other mother named you after a lotus blossom. They bloom in the water. Did you know that every day at dawn lotus flowers rise up from the mud and greet the sun?"

"They do?"

"They do. This whole situation has been terrible for you, I know. You've had a lot of the mud, so to speak. But you're like the lotus, my good girl. You're strong. You'll rise above it. I just know you will."

"Yes. I will," she said, softly, and almost in a whisper. But still, she said it, then nodded, and even smiled.

She didn't say anything more, though, and for the moment, I didn't want to push her into a long discussion she might not have been ready to have yet. "If and when you ever want to talk more about it," I told her, "I'm here, I love you, and I'll listen. So will your Dad."

Liana gave me a bigger smile. "Okay, Mom."

For the moment, that was that, but for certain, one day this discussion would be continued. It was enough for now that Liana knew the truth.

———◈———

Valentine's Day itself fell on a Saturday that year.

The doorbell rang in the middle of the morning. Jonathan had sent me a big bouquet of pink, red and white roses. I had gotten a large red heart filled with chocolates for him and smaller ones, along with little silver heart-shaped lockets, for each of my girls. They found the presents waiting for them at their places around the kitchen table when they sat down to lunch.

Then the bell rang again just as lunch was finishing up.

"Who could that be?" I wondered, and went to answer the door.

To my astonishment, the Nugents were on our front doorstep. All four of them. Howard the banker husband, Sofia the pain in the butt, and their two impossible children, Jack and Cecilia. Cecilia was holding a brown box, about one foot square, with a red sequined ribbon on top of it.

"Oh. If it isn't the Nugent family. Hello there. To what do I owe the pleasure?" I deadpanned. I did not swing open the door and let them in. Let them remain outside in the cold and the snow.

"If we could just have a few moments of your time," balding Howard Nugent said to me. "We've got something we'd like to say to you and your husband and children."

I didn't know if I should open the door wider or slam it in their faces and stood there, undecided.

Jonathan had come up behind me and heard some of what Howard had said. "Just for a minute," he told them. "And if there's anything inappropriate said by any one of you, out all of you go."

Howard sighed. "Fair enough."

They sat down in our living room, three on the couch and one on an easy chair, and that happened practically over my dead body. I was still furious at them. The girls came in from the kitchen but did not sit down, just stood by their father and me, like there were battle lines being drawn, us here, them there. Holly still had her arm in a sling. None of us trusted the Nugents as far as we could throw them.

"We want to apologize to you," Howard began. "All of you. Especially Holly. I realize that my wife and children have said and done some terrible things to you. *They* might have thought that was okay, but *I* never did. I didn't know how bad it had gotten until these two," he gestured towards his children, "went so far as to get expelled from school for a week over it. For violence against Holly, yet. I'm so ashamed."

"You were right all along," Sofia said to me in a soft tone that wasn't like her. "That was a wake-up call for Howard, and me, too. I wasn't setting the right example for my children by saying those awful things to you, Belinda."

"We're sorry we hurt you," Jack said sheepishly to Holly, unable to meet her gaze and looking down at our rug.

"Yes, sorry," Cecilia nodded. "Our allowance is even going to be docked until we finish paying for your doctor's bills for your arm. It might take us until July."

"Good," Holly grinned. She wasn't giving them an inch.

"I suppose that will teach you," I added. "You're lucky we didn't file an assault complaint with the police against you two kids. There's been a little too much hate coming towards us from you Nugents, and for far too long."

"Not from me," Howard assured us. "I won't stand for any more of it coming from my family, either. For my children to get expelled for hurting you, Holly, that had me mortified. It was the last straw."

"We, um, brought you something," Cecilia spoke up, almost shyly. Howard must have really read all three of them the riot act for his daughter to suddenly be acting so meek.

So nice, almost.

Only almost, probably.

Or possibly, and hopefully, not.

Cecilia held out the box with the red ribbon on top towards Holly.

Holly, of course, couldn't easily take it with only one good arm and the other one still in a sling. It wasn't that large a box but it was still too much for her to handle. "Liana, could you get it?" She asked her sister.

"Sure." Liana took the box from Cecilia.

Before she could open it, a small noise could be heard coming from inside. It sounded a bit like a whimper.

"What's that?" Bonnie said.

"Is it alive?" Holly asked. Her expression suddenly shifted from guarded to slightly excited.

I remembered something I'd overheard, had a feeling I already knew, and in spite of myself, started to smile.

Liana sat down on the floor beside the box, lifted the top open, and up popped the curious head of a sweet little tan-colored Cocker Spaniel puppy.

"Oh," breathed Bonnie, enchanted at once. She got down and joined Liana on the floor, reached into the box, and picked him up, cradling him in her arms like she had once held the babies in her orphanage.

"Let me see," Holly said, also sitting down beside the other two. Her eyes were shining. "Is this for real? He's for us?"

"For real," Cecilia told her.

"Our dog had pups a couple of weeks ago," Jack explained. "Since our dad says we need to start becoming decent people or else, we decided to give one to you."

Holly looked toward Howard and gave him a nod. "I like the 'or else part, Mr. Nugent.'"

She didn't add that *it was about time you did something, sir,* but she was probably thinking it. I know I was.

"The puppy is old enough to go to a new home now," Cecilia added. "He's eight weeks old. Did you know? Puppies can't go to new homes right away. They have to wait until the time is right and they're ready, or we would have brought him over sooner."

"We thought," Sofia said, "you O'Malley children might like to have a dog."

"We'd love one," Holly, finally looking utterly enthused, declared, and broke into a great big smile.

"They're often, I've found," Sofia added, "better companions than people."

"It's the least we can do," added Howard, "especially after everything that happened."

"Let's call him Lucky O'Malley," Liana suggested, reaching over and petting the little pup, who was still in Bonnie's arms. "He *is* lucky. To get to live here."

Well, that sure warmed my heart!

My girls and Jonathan, who squatted down on the floor to scratch the little puppy's ears, were delighted with Lucky. So was I.

Maybe it was time to give my neighborhood nemesis an inch.

"I'm sorry too," I said to Sofia. "For that whole incident with the ice cream."

"My fault," Sofia admitted, and it was her turn to look down in shame. "For provoking you in the first place."

"I'm not," Bonnie looked at her and said, "Viet Cong."

"Is *that* what you called her?" Howard demanded of Sofia.

She nodded, while her husband hid his head in his hands. He seemed mortified beyond all recognition.

They were all being so contrite, and it was so astonishingly out of character. It was easy to believe that maybe the two children had turned over a new leaf after their father lambasted them, but *Sofia?* She'd probably be up to her old tricks again within a fortnight, or even sooner. God help us at the next meeting of the PTA.

Well, we could hope for the best. Maybe this really was the start of a change in a good direction.

And if I wanted to, I could make an effort to mend matters, too. Right away. I could even try to turn this uncomfortable visit around and reshape it into a little party. It wouldn't be that hard, and after all, this *was* Valentine's Day, a time to bring people together. It wasn't a day where normally I could have expected to have four embarrassed guests sitting in my house with such glum faces.

"You know what? I've already made two dozen pink Valentine's Day cupcakes," I told everyone. "Why don't I bring some in here for all of us to share?"

Cecilia brightened for the first time since she'd arrived and said, "Hey, I like the sound of that!"

"So do I," her brother agreed. He also finally managed to allow a small grin to appear on his face.

Even Howard looked a bit happier at the thought of refreshments. Sofia only gave a tiny nod, which was probably about all she could muster in the way of affirming the plan, and yet, she did affirm it.

I went into the kitchen to get the cupcakes out of the refrigerator and arranged them on a red, pink and white holiday platter with a design of Valentine hearts. This was the least I could do. The puppy was making my girls so happy. After all they'd been through, a little dog to love could only be good for them.

Maybe this peace with the Nugents might just last. Perhaps this, what Howard was insisting upon, was even how parents could begin to stop bullying in its tracks, I thought. When someone like Howard put his foot down and made sure his family knew that it just plain *wasn't all right* to treat other people badly, it could possibly have a positive lasting impact, with the others knowing that it simply would not be tolerated for them to behave inappropriately on his watch. It might spark a new beginning.

Might.

I brought the treats back into the living room and passed the platter around, along with some pink paper plates.

It was still too awkward and silent a gathering.

Jonathan took action to remedy that. He went over to the stereo and put a favorite Elton John record onto the turntable.

When the irresistibly bouncy song "Crocodile Rock" began to play, who would have believed it? The five kids, complete with Liana holding Lucky in her arms, first started singing along, then almost as one, got up together and began to dance.

The End

Author's Note

Hello there and greetings from New York City!

Thank you so much for reading CHILD OF SECRETS FROM AFAR. I hope you had as much fun reading it as I've had creating it, and if you have, please be an absolute darling and leave a review on sites like Goodreads, or wherever booksellers and book lovers meet online. You can't imagine how much reviews help authors.

I always remembered the day that the very first Operation Babylift flight crashed in Vietnam. I was thirteen years old, and it was on the news for several days, along with broadcasts about the fall of Saigon. It couldn't have been more horrific.

But there was some good news. Although that crash came with many, many casualties, there were also 176 survivors.

Some of the most heartbreaking stories about the Operation Babylift children were those that came to light somewhat later. A few of the kids turned out to have parents back in Vietnam, ones who had wanted to send them to freedom in the United States, and when those children got here, they were bereft and cried to go home.

I've also heard countless stories of Asian or Black children, often from overseas, were adopted by loving White American families, had terrific parents, and yet felt like they stuck out like sore thumbs in their new predominantly White communities. Their adoptive parents, good people who weren't racists at all and strove to live in a manner that was "color-blind," didn't initially realize anything like that would happen, but it did.

Having once upon a time been bullied myself, not due to race but simply for being "the new kid" at two horrifically run private schools, I know what being in the crosshairs of a bully feels like, and realize all too well how much it is *still* going on, and *still* needs to be stopped. Not just for adopted kids, either. For all of them.

So with these many matters in mind, one fine winter day, when it was too cold for me to go gallivanting around outside like I usually do,

I came up with this story, set in 1975 and 1976, of a very nice woman called Belinda O'Malley, her wonderful husband Jonathan, gutsy daughter Holly, and their two newly adopted children from Operation Babylift, renamed Bonnie and Liana. One of their Vietnamese daughters is forthcoming about her past and background. The other is anything but. Then situation starts to go berserk when the family realizes that one of the girls is being targeted by someone for reasons unknown...and, of course, it just happens to be the child they know the least about.

Thanks again for reading CHLD OF SECRETS FROM AFAR. I would welcome the chance to connect with you and hear how you liked it. You can feel free to contact me through my website, www.carolynsummerquinn.com[1]. Keep smiling, and if you possibly can, try to do some good for somebody today. As I'm sure you already know, kindness never fails to count as a whole lot of wonderful to everyone lucky enough to be on the receiving end of it. Go forth and spread it around.

To life!

Best Regards, Happy Trails, and Lots of Love and Light,

CAROLYN SUMMER QUINN

---

1.   http://www.carolynsummerquinn.com

ABOUT AWARD-WINNING AUTHOR CAROLYN SUMMER QUINN

CAROLYN SUMMER QUINN, Author, Fine Art Photographer, and Winner, to date, of *SIXTEEN* writing awards, grew up singing show tunes in "good old" Roselle and Scotch Plains, NJ, a member of an outrageous and rollicking extended family. She has a B.A. in English and Theater/Media from Kean University and now delights in having escaped from the Jersey suburbs and lives in New York City.

She is the Author of ten books: the non-fiction theatrical biography *Mama Rose's Turn;* the middle-grade children's books, *Keep Your Songs in Your Heart* and *Now and Forevermore Arabella;* and seven delightful cozy mysteries, *The Final Comeuppance, Cloudy with a Chance of Answers, Backstabbed on Broadway, Vanished on the Vaudeville Circuit, A Charm Without a Chain, The Hollywood Backlash Moon,* and now this one, *Child of Secrets From Afar.*

Carolyn says that she always tries to incorporate the message into her writing that, "You just never know what tomorrow might bring." May it bring you something wonderful! You can find her at her website, www.carolynsummerquinn.com[2].

---

2.   http://www.carolynsummerquinn.com

Books By Award-Winning Author Carolyn Summer Quinn

Cozy Mysteries:
Child of Secrets From Afar
The Hollywood Backlash Moon
A Charm Without a Chain
Vanished on the Vaudeville Circuit
Backstabbed on Broadway
Cloudy with a Chance of Answers
The Final Comeuppance

*Nonfiction Biography of the Theatrical Legend
Who Inspired the Musical GYPSY:*
Mama Rose's Turn: The True Story of America's
Most Notorious Stage Mother

Middle Grade Children's Books:
Now and Forevermore Arabella
Keep Your Songs in Your Heart: A Story of Friendship and Hope
During World War II